Kasian Publishing
P.O. Box 211205
Eagan, MN 55121
www.KristinVanRisseghem.com

Cover design by Marya Heiman, Strong Image Editing
www.StrongImageEditing.com

Author photograph by Jessica Krueger Photography,
www.JessicaKruegerPhotograhy.com

Graphics Contributors, Theresa Knight/BigStockPhoto.com.

To my friends. You all inspire me.

PART I

Chapter 1

A staccato trumpet blast announced the exact moment when the change of seasons occurred. The double oak doors swung open with great ceremony, and King Oberon waltzed into the throne room, a glowing, pale blue scepter in his hand. His green robes flowed behind him, reminding me of a rolling prairie, billowing out behind him. His crown was entwined with white branches, and giant, dark green wings hung loosely around his body. He was the perfect picture of royalty.

Oberon silenced the horns with a wave of his massive hand. "Winter has ended," the Summer Fairyland king declared. "Let us join in celebration for the start of summer. May this exchange bring a bounty of wealth, growth, and prosperity."

The scepter now burned green, and he raised it high above his head before turning and placing the long metal staff on the altar near his throne.

On cue, flutes, fiddles, and drums raised an upbeat tempo, and the court exploded into song. Couples danced with their arms flowing around each other, and lone bodies swayed to their own beat. Some of the guests fluttered their wings, others cocooned themselves. House brownies streamed into the massive hall bearing plates of candied fruits, breads, and meats which they set on the royal table, which was already decorated with tall vases overflowing with fresh wildflowers. The delicious aroma of cheeses and buttery pastries wafted the air on the far side of the room.

I, on the other hand, stood alone with my back pressed against the wall and my fists clenched. The party would go on well into the night, but I had no intention of staying. I turned and blew out the candle sconce, needing to drape myself in darkness, then I wrapped my long, light green wings around my body. When I wasn't at a festival or party, I kept my wings hidden—unlike the fairies who chose to display them. The truth was that Fairies didn't need wings to fly, since we used glamour for that. Our wings only really need to come out when we experienced intense emotions.

I was almost out the door when my name was called. "Sidelle?" King Oberon's hand reached for me, caught my arm. "Where do you think you're slinking off to? Come and dance."

My nostrils flared. "Yes, Your Highness." I walked the few steps to the dais and placed a kiss on my father's cheek. Out of the corner of my eye, I saw the center of the scepter pulse to a soft green. "Just one. And then I'm outta here."

The king sighed with resignation. "I don't understand why you can't be a normal daughter. One who likes music and dances."

I shrugged, and he placed his hand on the small of my back, leading me to the center of the room. Multi-colored gowns and feathered masks parted before us like the sea.

"I do," I whispered, then inclined my head toward the onlookers. "Just not with all this."

"I wish you'd make friends with the nymphs and

pixies I send you from court."

A lone flute played the first notes to a popular song, and some of the crowd lost interest in us. Instead, they turned back to watch the musicians or join in the dance.

"I can make my own friends," I told him for the millionth time. "I'm not going to fabricate friendships just to appease you." I bowed gracefully, preparing for the dance. "Besides, I have Brea."

He nodded reluctantly. "Yes, you have Brea. But you are a Lady of Summer. You need to have more than *one* friend." He opened his arms and I stepped into them. We swayed to the slow tempo, letting our wings extend to their full height.

"Maybe I don't want any," I told him.

His eyes rolled toward the ceiling. "What am I going to do with you?"

"Nothing."

"I must do *something*." The Summer king guided me into a quick spin, and my olive gown swirled around my legs, followed by my wings. He grabbed my hand and waist when I teetered, close to losing my balance. "Do you have a special someone?"

I glared, righting myself. "This again? Father, I am *not* having this conversation with you."

"There are plenty of nobles who would love to have your hand in marriage—"

Enough was enough. "I'm not ready," I snapped, stepping out of his grasp. I grabbed my green-feathered mask, meaning to fling it to the ground, but it caught in the waves of my black hair instead, cutting short my dramatic intent. "And don't you *dare* try arranging anything. I want to live life on my own terms."

"It's customary for all members of the Royal Court to have a lifelong partner. You should settle down—"

"I have eons before I must marry." I stuck one hand

on my hip. "I don't understand why you keep insisting. We're immortal. There isn't any rush."

"As you wish." Oberon turned from me, but he always had to have the last word. "For now," he tossed over his shoulder as he stalked back to his throne, leaving me in a sea of brightly colored fairies.

I adjusted the mask to cover my face then stormed out of the masquerade, stewing over his last statement about marriage. I firmly believed someone would enter my life when the time was right, but until then, I would live on my own terms. I didn't need a fairy at my side, despite what my father said. In spite of my objections, every few hundred sundowns he raised the topic again, then set off on some fairy hunt to marry me off. So far I'd managed to squash all requests.

As far as my only having one friend, I saw absolutely nothing wrong with that. It had to be better than faking friendships with fairies that were only there because my father had instructed them to be there—or because they thought it would help their court status.

The lush gardens around Aestas Castle had begun to sprout, and their vivid colors glowed in the moonlight. Small flowers poked through the ground, and tree branches thickened with fresh buds. The soft new grass shoots invited me to touch them, so I removed my lace slippers, enjoying the squishy terrain beneath my bare feet. Encouraged by the warm breeze, I peeled off my shawl and let it fly into the wind.

As I walked the pathway toward the Wild Forest, sprites flew past, intent on cleaning the many statues. Some waved, others bowed toward me, and though I was in a hurry, I smiled back. In the distance, the moonlight shimmered like white magic on Lacus Pond. Every once in a while, something splashed on the surface, meaning the merfolk and water nymphs were probably frolicking. Goblins and gnomes romped the wooded grounds, scrounging for food and causing mischief, but I paid no attention to them.

The only thing on my mind was getting to my secret spot in the woods. I craved the peaceful atmosphere, away from prying eyes and fake smiles. In the woods I could be myself. I could say whatever thoughts crossed my mind. No one ever answered me, but that was okay.

When I finally arrived at my destination, I nestled onto the chair I'd fashioned a few seasons ago. The oak had stood solidly against the harsh winds and rain that sometimes pelted the area.

Yes, I was a fairy. But my life was not all about unicorns, rainbows, and parties, though—out of duty—I attended every royal event, no matter the size. There was hardly a night when something wasn't going on inside the castle or in the city of Aestas, whether we were throwing a royal festival or cheering up a pixie who had accidentally broken a flute. I was well aware that my father hated the sullen behavior I displayed whenever we received guests or listened to the problems of his subjects, but I never deviated. I had always been true to myself, and I knew deep down that the true me didn't quite fit in at Aestas Castle or at the royal outings. I much preferred to be in the forest. Alone.

In the peace and quiet of my favorite place, I remembered back to the celebration my father had thrown when I'd entered my fifth season. The whole city had been invited, of course, and all members of court had attended. I had been showered with gifts. Only one present still stood out in my memory, though. That was the gift which had shown me what I really was.

My one and only real friend, Brea, had given me parchment paper and some colored quills, and I'd used them to draw. Father discovered what I was doing, and though he wasn't angry, he seemed shocked that I could create pictures without glamour. But what choice did I have? When I was born, he'd sealed my magic. Since I was a Lady of the castle, it was important that I act properly. I couldn't be seen as a failure or someone who mistreated power. As a child I couldn't understand my powers or how to use them, so he'd kept them from me until I got older.

Brea's father hadn't sealed her glamour, so she taught me a few things over the seasons. One afternoon after that fifth birth's celebration, we sat in the garden, and I drew make believe worlds in which square towers loomed over the horizon and carriages moved without the aid of horses. On one side I swirled a lake of deep blue water, and on the other I created a vast green countryside. Brea guessed it was supposed to be a park, and she asked where it was since she'd never seen anything like it in Fairyland. When she told me my lake looked more like a fire pit, she was smiling. That's when she showed me a trick.

She held my hand palm side up, then cupped hers over mine. With her eyes twinkling, she said, "fire" then moved her hand away. Just like that, a green flame appeared, dancing in the center of my palm. Then she turned my wrist and said, "parchment" while tapping the area of water I had sketched on the paper. I stared in fascination as the flame transferred from my hand and hovered above the drawn lake like a sun.

Just then, the wind howled. It blew the green flame across the parchment and onto the grass. Real fire erupted and spread through the grass, hopping swiftly from branches to trees. Panicked, we flew to the castle for help and screamed the news to the first fairy we saw. Horns sounded, and a flurry of pixies and house brownies rushed to the garden. We ran back to watch, and my father materialized ahead of us. He snapped his fingers, and just like that the fire extinguished. Everything was as it had been before, with lush green grass and full flowering trees, though a charred stink lingered in the air.

It was then that my glamour training started. It was done under my father's guidance, and practiced in private. I guess he realized that my ignorance might be less dangerous than keeping me in the dark.

Chapter 2

The memory faded from my mind as I leaned down to replace my slippers. Just as I slipped my chilled toes in, a branch snapped behind me. My wings unfurled, startled by the sound, but I assumed it was just a sprite, climbing in a tree someplace nearby. When I heard nothing else, I contracted my wings and conjured my glamour, smiling to myself. I had come a long way since my first lesson.

As the glamour rose within me, my body tingled from head to toe, and my fingers pulsed, waiting to release my wishes. I focused, instructing the earth to open into a shallow pit then arrange wood fragments into a triangular stack. When all was prepared, I swept my hand over it and sent the green light. With the passing of seasons, and many days spent practicing, I had mastered fire. The green flames quivered in the slight breeze, not touching the twigs but casting a dancing light.

I stared into the glow, contemplating my current situation. If my father took matters into his own hands and forced me into a marriage, could I—

Another twig snapped much closer, and my skin prickled with alarm. My wings emerged from my back again, flapped twice, then slowed, fluttering slightly.

"Who's there?" I demanded, scanning the dense forest. "Come out. Slowly. I'm armed and I will—"

Leaves rustled nearby and more branches snapped. Something approached from the direction of the pond. I stood my ground and materialized a bow and an arrow, squinting into the darkness to focus my vision. I saw a hand wrap around a branch just a few feet away and took aim, waiting. The shadow unfolded like a curtain, revealing a head, then a torso, and finally a pair of long, lean legs. They belonged to a young, male fairy in a blue tunic.

"Hello," he said quietly, speaking in a low, deep voice. Even in the dark I saw his eyes on me. "I'm sorry. I didn't mean to scare you."

I rolled my shoulders back, standing tall, and pointed the silver tipped arrow at his chest. "You didn't." My wings twitched, always on guard. "I don't scare easily."

"You shouldn't be out here alone." He stepped forward but kept his wings hidden from view. The strangest sensation came over me when he spoke. Somehow his voice resonated in my bones and wrapped around me like a blanket.

"Says you," I said, matter of fact, "who is also alone in the forest."

"Yes," he said, sounding amused. He took a few more steps toward me, but I didn't move. "So I am."

I adjusted my grip on the bow. "Don't—"

"I'm not here to hurt you, My Lady." Very slowly he reached out and lowered the tip of the arrow, watching my reaction as he did so. I was too surprised to object. "I saw the flames and came to investigate."

My Lady? Why would he have called me that? How did he know me? I didn't recognize him, and I thought I knew all the Summer fairies.

"Who are you?" I demanded, lowering the bow but keeping it notched. He didn't seem to mean me any harm, but I stayed alert.

"No one. I'm just passing through."

When he turned toward me, the light from the fire revealed his exquisite features. Straight black hair framed a square, handsome face, accenting the piercing blue of his eyes. The chest he partially hid beneath his tunic was beautifully sculpted, and he was tall, towering over me; my head came to just under his chin.

"You don't have a name?"

"What are you doing out here all alone?" he asked, scanning the area and avoiding my question. "You're far from the city's borders."

"I know where I am."

"You must live in the city if you know this area well." He raised an eyebrow and slid his hands into the front pockets of his tan breeches. "Come here often?"

I wasn't about to let him grill me with twenty questions. "I think you need to move on. Especially since you're 'just passing through'."

"Of course." His smile was brief and apologetic. "I will leave you to . . . whatever it was you were doing." Without another word he brushed past me and headed deeper into the forest.

I stared after him, bewildered by the faint, cold feeling that lingered in his wake. It was odd that I had never seen him before, though I didn't know everyone in the city. He definitely didn't live in the castle, because I would have seen him there. On the other hand, maybe he was a recluse—like me—and didn't attend the festivities. For his sake, I hoped Father never found out that one of his subjects hadn't appeared at court when a royal decree had gone out.

I was intrigued. In all my seasons coming to this

spot, I had never seen another fairy venture this far from the castle and into the forest. It wasn't safe for them. It wasn't safe for me either, but my glamour was more potent than theirs because of my stature, which was third in line to the Queen Mother of Aestas.

That was another reason why my magic had been sealed in my earlier seasons. When I was about ten seasons old, father had explained to me what my rank meant. In the line of successions, if something happened to my mother, the queen, I would assume her title. For as long as I could remember, my grandmother, the Queen Mother, had ruled. In fact, she'd held the position for as long as father had known her. When I asked father more questions, he waved them off, telling me not to worry about the complicated succession rules. Evidently the status hadn't changed since the start of the seasons, and maybe not even before that.

Fairies have existed since before time was measured. Even before I came to understand the concept of eternity, the only measurement of time we counted was the number of changes of seasons. I remembered telling Father on my sixteenth season that nothing could last forever, but he had corrected me. He said 'fairies are forever.' At the time, I'd pondered the idea and eventually replied, 'for all of eternity.'

And that was how we came to call ourselves Eternals.

Chapter 3

I looked around my secret hideaway, strangely uncomfortable. The male fairy had somehow poisoned the place, making me want to scout a new location. I smothered the flame and swept my hand to return everything to the way it had been. New blades of grass now stood where others had lain flat, and the wooden chair came apart as sticks and branches moved back to their original places.

I glanced toward the pond, decided against going that way, then headed in a different direction, walking farther away from my home but staying in Summer. Rustling movements of elfin cats, water kelpies, and various insects surrounded me as I walked deeper into the forest. I called a flame to my palm, letting the green light illuminate the path for me. A blue shimmer in the air caught my eye, slowing my pace, and I stepped gingerly through the underbrush. Trying not to make any noise, I pulled aside the branches of a dense shrub and peeked through.

The small clearing before me opened into a vast, divisive canyon, and the other side of the ravine was covered entirely by a cloudy haze. I had heard of the Mist, but I'd never seen it before and had no idea it was that close to the city. The Mist surrounded Summer and Winter, moving almost like a living, breathing creature, but it never interfered with the Scepter exchanges. Any other time, the Mist could harm fairies if you weren't careful. You could get lost and never be seen again.

Nevertheless, the swirling clouds felt eerie, and my mind screamed at me to leave this place and never return. My wings twitched, eager to take me away, but some kind of force held me in place.

I tried to recall what had brought me here initially. Ah, yes. The glint of something blue.

I checked the area around me for any threat before I moved out onto the plateau, but apparently I didn't look hard enough. As soon as I stepped a little farther in I spied the stranger I'd met earlier. He sat on the edge, his long legs dangling over the side. The leather wrapped hilt of his sword peeked out from a black scabbard that crossed his muscular back.

I advanced on him as quietly as I could, not wanting to disturb him. I wasn't sure why I thought I shouldn't intrude, though. After all, he had stolen *my* safe place.

"I know you're there," he said, staring into the Mist. "I heard you as soon as you broke through the line of bushes."

"Oh, um . . ." My cheeks reddened and I searched for something intelligent to say. Unfortunately, all I came up with was, "Is . . . is this where you were headed?"

"No." He finally glanced up. When he saw I was watching him, his hands cupped something, then quickly slid whatever it was into his pocket.

"Can you not cross the canyon?" I asked. I walked to the edge and kicked a pebble, sending it into the pit, but I never heard it hit bottom.

"I don't know," he admitted. "I've never been so far

into—"

My green eyes met his blue ones, asking.

"I'm a long way from home."

"Maybe there's a bridge," I suggested. I craned my neck, looking either for a way over the canyon, but saw nothing. "You could use glamour to make one, or you could just fly across." Turning back toward him, I almost slipped. I threw out my arms for balance then kicked off my slippers. "I hate these stupid things."

He chuckled at my clumsiness. "Glamour doesn't work in the Mist. It may be sketchy even being this close. Didn't you know that?" His long legs kicked the side of the plateau. "Doesn't matter. I'll make my way around it."

I didn't miss the fact that he'd laughed at me, but he was full of interesting information. And no, I hadn't known glamour didn't work there. I suppose I should have, but there was no reason for me to know. No one ever ventured into the Mist on purpose.

"*Around* the Mist?" I asked, confused. "It stretches for many sun ups and downs." I frowned. "Actually, does it even end?"

He shrugged, still staring off into the gray fog. "I have all eternity to find out."

"When you put it that way." I let my breath out slowly. "Why did you leave home?" I blurted out, then I slapped my hand over my mouth.

"I'm sorry. You don't have to answer. I was just curious. I didn't mean to pry."

His handsome face twisted with something like disgust. "I'm just so sick of all this, you know?" He shook his head then scanned me from head to toe. One corner of his mouth curled briefly, but he didn't look like he was really laughing. "No, you definitely don't know what I mean. From the look of you, you live for parties, dressing up, and—"

"You don't know me!" I huffed, sweeping my hands down the front of my gown. "You think that just because I look like this I couldn't possibly understand? You have no idea." I scowled right back at him and pinched the stiff material clamped to my waist. "I wear this because my father tells me to. Otherwise, I wouldn't be wearing anything so extravagant. I mean, have *you* ever had to wear one of these?"

"Uh . . . no."

"Then you can't say anything." I glared at him until he looked away. Having won that round, I felt a little silly. Why I had gotten so upset with a complete stranger? Why did it matter what he thought? I changed direction. "Are you going to tell me your name now?"

"Are you?"

How irritating. Couldn't he answer a single question without asking another one? "I asked first."

"Fine," he finally said, softening at last. "It's Finnegan." He tilted his head and squinted my way, then patted the ground, motioning for me to sit.

I hesitated, then hiked up my skirt and plopped down next to him. It made no sense to argue with him, after all. "I'm Sidelle," I said, smoothing out my skirt. "What are you doing out here?"

"Exploring."

I lifted one brow and regarded him as if he were crazy. "In the Wild Forest then into the Mist? Are you on a death mission?"

He shrugged, not smiling. "It's how I get my kicks."

I became aware that I hadn't heard the sound of a single bird or animal since I'd arrived here. It made me wonder what kinds of predators lived in the Mist. Out here, beyond the shelter of the forest, the sky was black, but the grayish haze provided a vague light. I conjured a green fire, but it sputtered out. Using more glamour, I threw a fire ball and sent it floating over the canyon, close to the Mist side. It flickered, and I pulled it toward the center of the ravine where it barely lit the area with a green hue.

"Won't your father wonder where you are?" Finnegan asked.

"Probably." I nodded. "He won't send the search party—"

His body tensed beside me. "Search party?" He shook his head violently. "No! No one can find me." He jumped to his feet then dragged me up and pushed me toward the forest. "You need to leave now!"

"Whoa." I righted myself before I could fall over. "Hold on. You can't tell me what to do. You don't own this spot." I pointed to the ground. "Last time I checked, this was my—"

"Fine. Then *I'll* leave." He stalked away, following the edge of the canyon, then stopped and yelled back, "And don't follow!"

"Follow you?" I shouted at his retreating back. "Who do you think you are? I wouldn't follow you if you were the last Summer fairy in Aestas!"

"Good!" came his reply.

He was the most obnoxious fairy I'd ever met. No wonder he was running away from something. With a personality like that, I bet he didn't have any friends.

I extinguished the firelight, blinked, and ended up in my bedroom.

Chapter 4

"Where have you been?" Brea demanded the moment I appeared in my room. "The whole castle is talking about what's going on! I've been dying to talk with you about it."

Brea and I were complete opposites in almost every way, but she had always been my best friend. She was the yin to my yang. Fairies' outer appearances were based on the color of their wings, and we both had rare, iridescent, green wings, and distinct, almond-shaped eyes of the same color. Because of that, we predominately favored green, and we wore a lot of it. Other than those features, we were the reverse of each other. She was short, her brown hair was even shorter, and she loved to hang out with everyone. I, on the other hand, was quite tall for my kind, and I wore my black hair long. Hanging out wasn't for me; I preferred to be alone.

She was obviously excited about something. I smoothed out my skirt so she wouldn't notice anything out of place, and hoped I hadn't been missed by anyone else. "About what?"

"The scepter exchange didn't go as planned," she told me, standing at the mirror beside me. Her fingers pulled through her hair, attempting to straighten it. "Apparently the Winter fairy representative messed something up and said a wrong word. Their Queen is furious and on a fairy hunt."

I picked up a comb and ran it through her short waves, helping with some fly-aways. "And that has to do with Summer . . . how?"

"They may have to re-do the exchange."

I stopped mid-stroke. "That's crazy! They've *never* done two so close together. Won't that mess up the seasons?"

"I'm not sure."

"How do they know something went wrong?"

"The scepter isn't glowing green anymore." She held up her hands and backed toward my bed so she could sit. "Now, I'm getting all this second or third hand, so I'm not exactly sure what the real story is, but you know how the Summer and Winter representatives have to memorize the poem?"

I nodded and sat next to her, draping my legs over the edge.

"Well, the Winter fairy interchanged two of the lines, and now everything is in turmoil! When Winter handed his end of the staff to the Summer rep, it was still blue. By the time Oberon announced the Season change, it had turned green for a while and then the orb faded to white. Oberon's frantic."

"I bet he is." With a sigh, I lay back on the massive canopy bed, hooking my hands behind my head. "So now we wait?"

"I don't know," she said, sprawling beside me. "I guess we'll know more later." She paused, and her tone sweetened. "So? Did you dance with any nice fairies?"

"My father?" I picked at a stray thread on the duvet.

"Doesn't count."

"Why not?" I teased, though my wings itched to come out. I didn't want to have this conversation with her. It was pointless. She understood my reasons—sort of—but still badgered me about it. Sometimes she could be even more intrusive than my father. "Because he isn't nice?"

"No, because he's family." She rolled over and stared at me until I faced her. "I can't believe you don't actually want to find a fairy to marry." She giggled. "Hey, that rhymes!"

I rolled my eyes. "Brea, you know why." I shook my head. "Just don't forget about me when you find your handsome prince."

She giggled again. Sometimes I envied her lightness, her way of enjoying just about everything—including the hunt for the right male fairy. Why couldn't I be more like her?

"You still believe in the fairy's tales?" she asked.

"Yeah, maybe I do."

"You know," she said, her eyes glazing over, "since you're kinda like a princess, the fairy you marry has to be a prince. I hope he's dreamy." She sighed then perked up. "Hey, where did you go this evening? I didn't see you."

"I left after I danced with my father," I said, staying vague. "You know I can't stand all the parties and dressing up."

"Aversion to dancing. Check. Aversion to meeting gorgeous Fairies. Check." She shook her head. "I just don't get you. But whatever. You are your own business." Her green eyes crinkled with her smile. "Well, I'm gonna fly now. I just couldn't wait to talk with you about all this, but now I wanna know more about what's happening!"

"Okay," I said. "See you later."

"Hugs!" And she vanished, leaving me with my bed to myself.

Hours later I opened my eyes and squinted against the sunlight streaming in through the windows. My entire body ached, and I decided a long soak in the warm spring was just what I needed. Maybe then I could actually make some decisions for my life. With a groan I rose, stretched, and headed out of my room. Down the hall was my bathroom, which had been built around a private spring. The lavender oils and amber fragrances which I used for special occasions stood beside the pool, and I poured in just the right amount before I slipped into the soothing water, my eyes closed.

Yes, I would live forever, but—though I wasn't about to admit it to anyone—I was aware that something in my life had to change. I couldn't keep going like this, flitting around and attending parties, listening to the same court gossip over and over again. What could I do? How could I break the monotony of it all?

The image of the dark-haired fairy by the Mist haunted my thoughts. Curious, I thought, that I would think of him just as I considered my future. *Finnegan*. A thought tugged at my brain, waiting to be released, and I reached idly for the perfume by my head.

"Lady Sidelle?" A Water Nymph poked her head out of the water, surprising me. I accidentally dropped the bottle, making a splash.

"Yes?"

"Your father wishes to see you." She dropped below the surface, and though I waited a moment or two, she didn't return with any further explanation.

So much for my relaxing day.

I dried off then dressed in a gold gown which I knew the king would approve. I had no idea what he wanted to talk to me about, but I had a sinking feeling. If he wanted to speak with me this early, right after the Exchange, it could not possibly be good.

A thought hit me, and I grimaced. What if—even after all my warnings—he'd found a "suitable" fairy for me to marry? I slowed my pace, though I knew he wouldn't like my being late. I couldn't push the awful sense of dread from my mind. My wings drooped. I stopped outside the throne room, drew in a deep breath for courage, then pushed opened the massive, double oak doors.

King Oberon grinned when he saw me. "Ah, Sidelle. Come. Come." He stood with open arms. "I am sure you have heard the news by now, yes?"

"Good morning, Father." I bowed before walking a few more steps to stand in front of him. "Yes, Brea told me, but I'm not sure if her facts were correct."

He chuckled. "I sometimes wonder where that fairy gets all her information. I'll have to look into that later." He still smiled as he cocked his head to one side, but I saw the strain in his expression. "Last night when I viewed the scepter, the color was still blue. Yellow had not taken over even though the exchange had been completed and the scepter had arrived in Summer." He puffed out a breath. "And if it doesn't turn green?" He shook his head. "Well, let's not ever wish that. That would mean having too long of a winter in the Ordinaries' realm."

"And you think it was the representative . . ."

He nodded. "I sent a message to Queen Mab, and she confirmed that the poem had been spoken incorrectly by her subject. *Our* representative said their part precisely."

I nodded, waiting.

"I don't need to go into details as to all she said and will do, but well, in a nutshell, the Winter fairy has fled. Her guards followed him until they lost him in the Mist."

"The Mist?" I echoed, puzzled. "I—"

"You will stay on the grounds," he ordered. "No wandering off until the culprit is found and taken back to Winter Court." He grabbed my shoulders and forced me to look at him. "Understand?"

"Yes." I nodded, then I shook my head slowly. I had to tell him. *Be brave.* "I . . . I think I met him. You see, I took a walk in the forest after our dance, and—"

"What?" His face reddened. "*Guards!*"

I stepped back from his rage, and a flurry of fairies swept into the room, dressed in full armor. Each wooden shield displayed the Aestas Castle crest: a thorn crown wrapped in green wings. The guards formed a single line and bowed in unison.

"My daughter will lead you to the last known location of the Winter fairy."

I gasped and looked at him, hoping for some kind of reprieve. There was no hint of one in his eyes. I thought of Finnegan and remembered how his departing words to me had been an order not to follow him.

What had I done?

Chapter 5

With no other choice, I led the knights to the edge of the plateau where I had last seen Finnegan. He was no longer there, of course. The guards spread out and swept the banks, but there wasn't a trace of the Winter fairy. Not even a hint of frost.

I hadn't known he was from Winter. I should have. I should've felt something *off* about him. Then again, I hadn't really registered him as a true enemy.

Maybe he wasn't even the fairy the Winter Queen Mab hunted.

We searched well into the sunrise, scouring every inch of the Forest and as close to the Mist as anyone dared. I'll admit that wasn't very far, though, because no one dared enter it. I really wanted to walk into its outer edge, but I didn't want to give my father any more reasons to scold me.

"This was the last location I saw him," I told one of the guards, pointing at the exact spot where we had sat, perched on the edge of the plateau. "He was right here before I returned to the castle." I frowned, working on the puzzle. "He can't hide, not if he really is from Winter. He'll weaken to the state of almost nothingness. The King will find him eventually."

"Over here!" a guard shouted. He was kneeling on the ground, pressing his hand to it. "I think I found something." I ran over with some of the others to see what he was talking about. "Feel this spot," he said. "It's cool to the touch even though we're in full sun." He looked up and scanned the area. "He has to be close. Fan out! We must find him."

The knights obeyed by searching every crater and crevice. They lifted boulders, swept away tree bows, and checked caverns for any additional signs.

"Go sweep the area around Lacus Pond," I instructed the head officer, deciding to take charge of the situation. Maybe then my father would see that I could be more than just someone's bride. "He can't be too far."

An idea formed in my mind, and I turned to face the sun. Digging deep inside myself, I pulled the glamour around me and focused on the elements. It took a lot of control to affect the elements—especially the sun and moon—but being a Summer Lady did have its perks, since I had more natural powers than most other fairies. I concentrated hard, feeling the sun penetrate my skin and pass through my wings until each ray surrounded me. Eventually I held them all, and ever so slowly they bent to my will. I asked them to warm the area in which we searched, to show us the way. Instantly, the light intensified around us, and sweat beads rolled down the knights' foreheads. Heat waves rose from the mist-dampened rocks, creating clear smoke in the air. It was so hot I flapped my wings to pull a breeze around me.

A light cough reached my ears.

"Silence, everyone," I commanded, and all movements ceased. "I thought I heard—"

Another cough echoed into the air.

I pointed behind me. "Go!"

The knights raced in the direction of the noise, then I

heard the sounds of yelling, grunting, and branches being snapped.

"Ah!" a guard exclaimed. "Found you! Hiding like a coward."

"It's not me," came the response. "You have the wrong fairy."

"No, I don't think so. Why else would you be here?" The commanding officer pushed a tall figure through the tree line and into my view. "Is this him?" he asked.

I fidgeted, saying nothing until Finnegan stood before me. Our eyes met, and I reluctantly nodded.

"You!" He fought to break free of the knights' tight grasps, twisting and yanking in their hands. "You turned me in? How could you? All I asked was to be left alone!"

"I—" I said helplessly.

Finnegan scowled, furious, then turned away. "Save it for someone who cares."

The captain of the knights grabbed the back of Finnegan's tunic. "We're taking you to the dungeon until your Queen can come for you," he informed him with a sneer. "There's no use resisting. You're outnumbered. You couldn't possibly take on this many knights. Not when the sun is draining you."

We returned to the warm comfort of Aestas Castle with a weakened Winter fairy in tow. The dungeons were deep underground, but I had never had a reason to go there before. I watched from the shadows as the knights dropped Finnegan's limp body onto the warm, hard ground then chained him with cuffs made of green vines. He frustrated their efforts by freezing the vines until they shattered.

The cell would not hold him. It wasn't made for someone from Winter. In fact, the dungeons were rarely used at all anymore. To live without the warmth of the sun's rays and moon for who knew how long would be enough torture for any Summer fairy.

"Has he admitted anything yet?" the King asked, bustling into the dungeon.

I turned myself invisible. I couldn't face either him or Finnegan.

A guard stood stiffly outside the cell. "No. Not a word."

"I see. Has he tried to use his glamour?"

"He's too weak."

Oberon waved his hand to dismiss the guard. "Leave. I would like to talk with him."

The guard looked flustered. "Your Majesty, I should stay—"

"Go," the king whispered. "I won't say it again."

The knight bowed reluctantly then disappeared.

King Oberon stepped through the solid dirt wall as if it wasn't there. "Your Queen is on her way to attend to you," he told the prisoner. His statement was met with silence, and I heard annoyance in my father's voice. "What? Nothing to say?" He paused. "Well, I'm sure she has ways to make you talk." He took a moment to catch his breath then went on, lowering his voice so I could barely hear. "I have to ask you a question, though. You met my daughter . . ."

Stunned at his change of direction, I moved closer to the door. Finnegan's blue eyes snapped open just in time for me to see him do it. So he *had* been listening.

"And on her life," Finnegan said in reply, staring directly at him, "I tell you that the Winter fairy you seek is not me. I did not attend this Season's Exchange. This is all a huge case of mistaken identity."

To swear on a fairy's life was serious. It was right up there with oaths. With that kind of declaration, Oberon *had* to believe him. My wings fluttered, and my stomach heaved with guilt. Maybe I had been wrong about Finnegan. I'd assumed—

"Sidelle?"

I flinched. He must have heard the rustling of my wings. My head snapped up, became visible, and I met my father's heated glare.

"Yes?" I squeaked.

"Is this the fairy you saw after our dance?"

"Yes, but—"

"Say no more. I believe both of you," he said, patting my shoulder. "However, I cannot have a Winter fairy loose in the castle. He will remain our guest here until his Queen arrives."

I bowed but was still confused. "Yes, sire, and I'm glad you believe me, but—"

He waved a dismissive hand. "Of course I believe you, Sidelle. You've never told me an untruth before, and you have no reason to start now. Besides, the scepter is burning a bright green now, so that means all is right in Summer again."

"Since he's not a prisoner," I said, staring at Finnegan, "may I have him moved?"

"To where?"

"I was thinking the southern tower. It gets direct sun, which would keep him safe if he tries to escape before Winter comes for him—"

"Excellent idea." Oberon nodded. "I'll have him moved. Immediately. He's to be escorted at all times by guards if he leaves the room, but I would prefer him to stay inside the southern wing."

My father had Finnegan relocated and gave him some clothes, but he made him a prisoner of the tower. A guard stood watch outside his door. Thankfully, the southern tower encompassed more than one room, since it was where honored guests of the court stayed. In fact, it was considered a privilege to stay in that wing. The windows overlooked gardens, rolling pastures, and cascading waterfalls, providing one of the best views our castle had to offer.

The precautions were taken because we truly didn't know what a Winter fairy could do to us. We also needed to keep him safe from a Summer fairy who might want to take him out. It made me sad that Finnegan had to be confined, but like my father said, it wasn't safe for him to wander free in Aestas. Once word spread through the city that Oberon had proclaimed the Winter Prince to be a guest, no one dared try anything and anger the king, but for now his presence represented a threat.

By the next sundown after Finnegan's move, I wanted to check on him. As the lady of the castle it was my duty. Of course, I was also pretty curious about him, and this time he couldn't walk away from me. I tapped on the door.

"Hello? May I enter?" I heard nothing for a moment, but as I raised my hand again to knock harder, I heard his muffled, "Yes."

The guard nodded then pushed the door open for me. Finnegan stood by the windowsill, gazing out. The room was in perfect order. No indentation was on the chaise cushions, and I didn't think the bed had even been slept in.

"I see you've made the space your own."

He didn't even look at me. "Why are you here?"

"You might show me some courtesy." My hands clenched at my sides. "I could have left you in the dungeon instead of having you moved here."

"It might be better for me in the cellar," he said quietly. "I'm not cut out to be in Summer this long."

He finally turned to face me and I stepped back, shocked. His skin had faded to a greyish color, his muscular body had lost some of its definition, and the twinkle in his blue eyes had completely vanished. *This is my fault.* I marched forward and reached to touch his arm, but stopped when he pulled away.

"Are you dying?"

"No, I don't think so, just weak." He frowned. "I think."

"Can't you just make this room cold or change it to a temperature that would suit you?"

"I could." He nodded, but he didn't look optimistic. "But that takes a lot of energy, and I don't know when I'll be back in Winter to recharge."

I glanced away. "Oh."

"Don't worry about it. I'm sure my Queen will fetch me soon."

"I came to see if you needed anything—other than a cold chamber, that is." I sat in one of the chairs, deciding to stay a little longer. "If you do, just ask. I'll see what I can do. Obviously the king—"

"Your father, *Princess*." I didn't miss the sneer in his voice.

"Yes," I said coolly. "My *father* told you not to leave the room unescorted. And I'm a *lady* of Summer court. I can escort you if I have some kind of guarantee that you won't hurt me."

He crossed his arms and glared. "If I wanted to hurt you, I would have done it in the Forest when no one was watching."

"Good point," I conceded. "So if you want something—"

He shook his head. "I don't get it. Why are you

being nice to me? Why now?" His eyes narrowed. "What do you want from me?"

"Well, the truth is that I feel bad about what I did."

"Don't bother."

My wings fluttered then lowered. "You don't know me. I *could* make your stay here miserable."

"Just leave me alone," he muttered. "I'm sure you have some party to get ready for."

"Why do you have to be like that?" I demanded. "I'm trying to be . . . oh, never mind. If you want to be alone, fine. Be by yourself. See if I care."

I slipped from the room without waiting for a response. Finnegan had gotten under my skin, and what upset me even more was that I'd let him.

Chapter 6

Three sundowns later, I found myself standing outside Finnegan's door again. Sure, he had been rude to me, but could I really blame him? He was imprisoned, weakened, kept away from his home, and was probably anticipating a severe punishment when he finally returned to Winter. The guard let me pass, and I knocked on the door. This time I didn't wait for a response. It was *my* castle, after all. I strode into the room with my head high.

"I brought your food. It's a peace offering for my rude behavior."

"Leave it on the table." He still stood in the exact same place, near the window. "And then you can leave."

I wasn't about to be so easily dismissed. I ignored him and settled myself on the chaise. "I thought you might like some company, since no one has come to visit. The least you could do is sit and have a conversation with me."

He glared at me through cold, narrowed eyes, and I sank deeper into the cushion, feeling powerless, then straightened, remembering who I was. I returned his gaze with daggers of my own. Eventually one of his feet moved, and he gave in. He casually walked over and took the chair opposite me. I smirked, having won that small battle, and wondered if there were any more cracks I could break in that icy exterior of his.

"What do you want to talk about?" he asked.

"Whatever is on your mind." I crossed my legs waiting for a response. "How are you holding up?"

"This is going to be a very short conversation." He looked away. "I have nothing to say."

"Fine. I'll start." I folded my arms, tired of walking on eggshells around him. "Why were you in the forest?"

My question was met with silence.

"Okay, let's try this," I said, deciding honesty might just be the best method of getting anything out of him. "I was out there because I like to get away from the court. You can't possibly understand the pressure that comes with all that. I hate it and don't want to do it anymore, but as you can guess, my father won't hear of it." I waved a hand to the side, putting a little drama into my tirade. "He wants to marry me off to someone, but I don't want that either. I don't know what I want, to be honest, but I feel like there's something else that I'm supposed to do with my existence. Besides, as Fairies we have eternity to be with someone, right?"

He stared blankly at me.

"You know what I mean?" I tried again. "Probably not. But I guess you are running from something, too. Why else would you travel into the Mist? And now that I know you're from Winter, and you're the first I've ever met outside of the Exchanges—"

"You talk a lot," he said.

My head snapped toward him. "You can speak!" I took a breath then launched into my long list of questions. "How long have you been in Summer? Is this your first time here? What have you been eating? Where have you been hiding? Wait. Scratch that last one. I get that you can't tell me, because then it wouldn't be a hiding place anymore. So tell me something else. What do you do outside in Winter when it's always cold? I can't imagine it would be like it is here, warm and sunny during the day, beautiful nights to have picnics, play games, and be outside."

I stopped, inhaled, then smiled at him, waiting for his replies.

He hesitated, then one corner of his mouth twitched. "That's a lot of questions. Do you want me to answer them now, or are you going to rattle more off?"

"Be nice." I pointed a strawberry at him, then plopped it into my mouth.

"I may've lost track of your questions, but here goes. No. Stuff. Here and there." He frowned, thinking. "I think that's the first group. As for the second set, well, we have the sun and moon, too. Yes, it's cold outside the castle, but we're used to it. It doesn't bother us. I don't know what a picnic is, and we don't play. Only young fairies have snowball fights, construct ice buildings, and go snow riding."

I nodded slowly, thinking through all the answers. Frankly, I was surprised to have received so many. "So what have you seen here that's different?"

"Unfrozen water."

"What's snow riding?"

"It's not what you think." He chuckled, lifting one dark eyebrow. "I can see you're trying to picture how one rides snow, but it's not like that. We make thick sheets of ice then ride them down the hills. It can get pretty brutal, because some cheaters use their glamour to steer and ram into others. We've had a few bloody . . . accidents."

"Sounds fun." I wasn't sure if I meant it or not. My voice stayed flat. "Sign this fairy up to be first in line to try that." I picked at the seat cover. "So are you going to tell me why you are in Summer?"

He looked away. "I needed to get away. I wanted to see what else was out there."

That sounded eerily familiar. "So you're kind of like me? Looking for more?"

"I guess you could say that."

He smiled for the first time, and the result was glorious. His whole face lit with it, the glint in his blue eyes danced, and his body seemed to almost glow. Something fluttered deep in my stomach at the sight, and I wanted to glance away, to hide the flush of pleasure that had just risen to my cheeks. But I couldn't.

Visiting Finnegan after dinner became my routine. Before that, I flitted around the castle, waiting for the sun to set so my time with him could resume. I couldn't go earlier, after all, because he rested during the peak time, when the sun was high in the sky.

After thirty sundowns, the novelty of housing a Winter fairy had worn off for the most part, so I heard fewer mutterings of those who questioned the King and their own safety. Finnegan never left the tower, and he had never even asked to leave. I actually thought most of Summer had forgotten about him, and I wondered why no one from Winter had come. Maybe they wanted to punish him. Or maybe he wasn't important to their Queen.

As usual, I wasn't like the rest of Summer. I couldn't get Finnegan out of my mind. There was more to him, and I wanted to know all of it. He was handsome even for a Winter fairy, with the most beautiful blue eyes, a muscular body, and soft jet black hair. I knew it was soft, because I touched it once—I didn't think he noticed. But he was also interesting. Through our evening visits he started to reveal more about himself and his dreams. I was mesmerized; convinced we were two single Fairies dancing to the same, slow song.

I spent so much time with him that Brea and I saw less and less of each other. She appeared in my room one day, tapping her foot, obviously upset. "What in fairies' green land are you doing? Why are you spending so much time with *him*?" I opened my mouth to answer, but she held up an admonishing finger and shook it. "Oh yes, I know where you've been all these days, so don't you dare speak an untruth!"

"It's not what you think," I said. "He's not at all what we assumed Winter fairies to be. They're not all violent and war loving."

She wasn't satisfied by my answer, but I could see she was intrigued. I sat on my bed and patted the spot beside me.

"What do you two talk about?" she asked, dropping onto the bed. "What could you both have in common that means you need to be up all night? I know what time you slink out of the room—or have you forgotten that the guard stationed outside the tower is a friend of mine?" She folded her arms and gave me a little wink. "Oh yes, he tells me you visit our guest and stay all night. He can hear your voices."

My jaw dropped. "Brea! We're not doing *that!* Obviously Summer does not mix with Winter." I knew the boundaries, and yes, I pushed them, but I didn't break them altogether. I shrugged. "Besides, he's . . . nice. He's been telling me about his home, and I've shared things about living here. We've come to an understanding, I think." *I hope.*

"You're falling for him. I know you are." She stared

into my eyes, trying to read me. "I've never heard you talk like this. You've never been so smitten about anyone."

I sat up and gaped at her. "I am not. I can't be. I'm not."

"Sure. Whatever. You keep telling yourself that, Sid. It's okay with me, you know. I've always wanted you to be happy, and if he makes that happen, then fine. *I* don't have to like him. I don't know him, and I won't judge. I trust *you*." She nudged my shoulder. "But please be careful who you give your heart to. That's all I'm saying." She nodded, looking pleased with herself. "And on that note, this matter is closed. Not unless you bring it up first, okay?"

That was a relief. I had been afraid this conversation would go on forever. "Thanks, Brea." I smiled.

She winked again. "No wings off my back."

But she'd given me something to think about, that was for certain.

Had I given my heart to Finnegan without realizing I was doing it? We had a fair number of rules around here, but the one no one ever broke was that Summer and Winter did not mix. I couldn't be with him. I knew that, but my brain wasn't talking sense. It kept throwing out objections. So I got to thinking . . . if I *did* love him, what'd be the worst that could happen?

Chapter 7

After forty more sundowns, a long procession of ice-covered carriages rolled to a stop outside the castle's gates. The pomp and circumstance of their arrival was overwhelming, and I watched in awe from my window. The event was as grand as an exchange parade, which was due to take place again in ten sundowns. The castle buzzed with excitement when the Winter guards finally came to retrieve our guest.

I was staring out my window when a Pixie appeared in my room. "My Lady?"

"Yes?"

"Your father has requested your attendance in the throne room. He said to take your time." She grinned. "He said Winter can wait until you're ready to see them."

I drew in a deep breath, trying to get my emotions under control. "Thank you."

It was time. I brushed my hair, used glamour to fix it into a braid, then labored over selecting a gown. All the time I was preparing, I thought about how much I'd miss having Finnegan around. I had gotten used to being near him. But if anyone found out that I was comfortable around a Winter fairy, the reaction wouldn't be good at all. If my father found out, he'd be furious. Then again, he *did* want me to marry . . .

Where did that idea come from?

Taking my time to ponder on that thought, I strolled through the tower and stopped outside Finnegan's doorway. It took a moment before I could go any farther, since I still felt shaken that I'd even entertained him as marriage material. Finally I knocked and strode in as I always did.

"Your guards are here to take you back to Winter," I told him.

"I know." He stared out the turret window. "Thank you, Sidelle, for keeping me company and for being . . . civil to me." His voice was low, and I heard something unfamiliar in it. Regret? "I don't imagine I'll ever see you again."

I lowered my eyes and blinked rapidly. I would not cry. "For what it's worth," I admitted quietly, "I'm sorry for turning you in, and I wish you didn't have to go."

"I know." He smiled, but his eyes didn't have that sparkle I'd come to know. "Hey. You look nice, Delle."

I blinked again, this time out of surprise. "What did you call me?"

He lifted one shoulder in a sheepish shrug. "I thought it was a good nickname for you. You and I have come a long way, and I didn't think we needed to be so formal anymore."

My cheeks burned, but I grinned. "I like it . . . Finn."

We both turned toward the door as it opened, revealing a tall Winter guard dressed in blue armor. He stepped over the threshold, and the room seemed to close in now that it contained his massive size.

Looking eternally bored, Finn kicked off the wall and marched toward the guard. "Let's get this over with," he said. "Take me back to Winter if you must."

The guard dropped to one knee, confusion in his expression. "Your Highness! You're their prisoner, sire? There must be some misunderstanding. I was sent to escort—"

"Highness?" Oberon asked as he appeared into the room. He glanced apologetically at me. "Sidelle, you were taking a bit too long, so I led the guard to our guest."

I barely heard him. I'd been staring at the guard, but now my gaze rose to meet Finn's. I pointed to the guard. "What is he talking about, Finn?"

He shrugged, but I knew him well enough by now— or at least I thought I did—to recognize the concern in his expression.

"You are a Lady of this court," he said, "and I am a Prince of Winter court." He cleared his throat. "You never asked, and I didn't tell. I didn't think it mattered."

This made no sense. Considering all the nights we'd sat in the cold quiet of his room, talking about our lives, our thoughts . . . "So you told an untruth?"

"Not a lie. I just withheld that part."

I gaped at him, one hand on my hip, not sure how to react to this revelation. "That doesn't sound much better, you know."

"Excuse me," the Winter guard interrupted, "but where is Cam?" He looked around the room then at my father. "I was told to bring the Winter representative back, but I have no authority to bring back the Winter Prince."

"This is the only Winter fairy we hold," the King said.

"So it's true?" I asked, making sense of the conversation at last. "You really *aren't* the one your Queen was looking for?"

He nodded.

"That means you told the truth about the exchange!" I exclaimed, then I threw my arms around Finn's neck and hugged him tight. That's when my father cleared his throat, and I remembered he was in the room. "I'm so glad it wasn't you," I whispered into Finn's ear before I stepped back and smoothed my green dress.

The guard bowed before Finn then before Oberon. "Since Cam isn't here," he said, "I expect I'll be on my way. Your Highness, will you be returning with us?"

"It's of no concern to you," Finn said, waving him away. "You may take your leave."

"As you wish." The guard nodded once, then he turned and walked out of the room.

As the door eased closed, Finn's eyes suddenly widened. "Wait!" he shouted.

The guard reappeared in the doorway. "Your Majesty?"

"I need a recharge. Staying here in Summer has almost drained me of my glamour."

Without another word, the guard stepped back into the room and extended his arm. Finn placed his fingers against the guard's hand, producing an intense blue light that filled the room. It pulsed a couple of times then disappeared. When the light was out, the guard bowed and left.

While all this was going on, I looked over at my father and noticed he was smiling. After the guard had gone, Oberon winked at me then disappeared. I had no idea what that meant. Confused, I stared at the spot where he'd stood just a moment before.

"So," Finn said, but I was still staring at the empty place in the room. I wondered what my father had seen—besides the hug—that might have warranted that kind of wink.

"Delle?"

My eyes went to Finn, but I didn't speak.

"Now that I'm no longer a prisoner of the tower, would you like to go outside with me?"

I nodded, mute.

"You know," he said, holding the door open for me to pass through, "I haven't been beyond these walls since I came to the castle seventy-five sundowns ago."

Knowing that he had been counting our sundowns together warmed my wings.

I led him through the castle and to the gardens. Once we were there, he closed his eyes and breathed in deeply, taking everything in—including his freedom. Eventually his lids opened, and he cupped his hands, producing a tiny blue flame between them. I knew what he was doing: quietly rejoicing that his glamour had been restored enough that he could conjure fire, one of the basic elements. My heart sank with guilt, knowing we had kept him confined all this time.

But the selfish truth was that I wouldn't trade the past seventy-five sundowns for anything. During them, I had learned so much about him, and he'd grown to know me. We'd connected on a level I hadn't had with anyone else, not even Brea.

"What would you like to do?" Finn asked, smiling broadly. "We need to do something. I want to celebrate my freedom."

"I'm still mad at you for not telling me you were a Prince," I told him.

"Oh? Come on. You can't be angry at me for that." He walked to my side and reached for my hand, but I snatched it away. "I didn't think it mattered. It doesn't."

"Yes, it does. I'm annoyed, actually. You should've been open and honest." I crossed my arms. "In all the time we've spent together, it never once crossed your mind that I might want to know about that part of your life?"

"It's only a small part. It's not what makes me who I am." This time he grabbed my hand and squeezed. The coolness of his touch swept up my fingers and arm. "I thought, you of all people, would understand that the title is just a title. Now come on. Show me something about Summer that I don't know."

With his gentle tug, my irritation vanished. We wandered to Lacus Pond, and I summoned a boat to the shore. It rocked gently at the edge of the water, and after Finn climbed in, he offered his hand to help me in. I grabbed for one of the oars, but he beat me to them.

Night fell early, and the willow wisps blinked in and out, creating a twinkle of lights in the darkness. The half-moon reflected off the water's glassy surface. Owls hooted all around, and the soft flutter of birds' wings joined the swirling hum of the cicadas, creating a soothing rhythm and a serene mood. We sat in silence in the little boat, floating around the pond. After a while I draped my upper body over the port side, letting my fingers skim the water's surface.

Finn's voice broke the silence. "I've never been on a boat before," he said. "It's nice."

"I wouldn't think so," I said, grinning, "since all your lakes are frozen. You said you wanted to do something you've never done, and I thought this would be perfect." I tilted my head. "You're doing just fine on those oars."

He chuckled. "You surprise me still, Delle."

I liked that, and I loved the sound of his chuckle, soft and smooth in the darkness. "I like my nickname, by the way." I held out my hands. "Here. I should row for a while."

"No, I don't think so."

"I can see sweat running down your face, Finn, and I

don't feel like hauling your body back to the castle. You should take it easy for a while." Ignoring his protests, my fingers twitched with glamour, and the oars continued rowing by themselves. "See? This is much better anyway. And now we can eat."

A wave of my hand brought us a wicker basket filled with fresh fruits, candied nuts, and meats. I'd kept the food simple and made sure it was everything I knew Finn could eat. Keeping him as a captive had given me some insight on what he could and couldn't digest, though I still wondered why he couldn't eat breads.

"These are my favorites," Finn said as he grabbed a handful of the sweet nuts. "They're so rare in Winter. When the snow and ice aren't thick, we're able to keep a small stock of these, but they're mostly saved for the Exchange dinners."

"I love fruits and cheeses. Do you have these?" I dropped a piece of kiwi in my mouth.

"All fresh foods are rare, except for meat. We have to thaw most of our meals then heat them until they're edible. But I'm not into eating fruits. I've never liked the sweet tastes." He leaned over and flicked water at me. "Is this what you call a picnic?"

"Yes, except usually we sit on the grass. This is a boat picnic."

"Yeah. That wouldn't work at home. It'd be pretty uncomfortable, sitting on the frozen ground and eating dinner."

I nibbled on a perfectly ripe mango. "Don't you live in the Winter castle? I mean, I figured you would, since you're a prince."

"Yes, and so the question is . . ." He circled his finger around the basket. "Why would I do this if I have a table?"

"Because it's fun, and it's different from being

inside, or at a banquet."

He kept his eyes on me while he popped a couple of sweet nuts into his mouth. The intensity of his gaze made me a little uncomfortable. I couldn't figure out what he was thinking.

"I can tell you enjoy picnics," he said, one corner of his mouth curling into a wry smile. "You've had a smile on your beautiful face since we arrived here."

Beautiful? I'm sure my cheeks went crimson at that. I looked down at my hands. "Yeah, picnics make me happy. I guess it's because they're so quiet and simple." The water rippled around the boat, daring me to look at him again. "You noticed I was smiling?"

"Of course. Why wouldn't I?"

I shrugged. "I didn't think it'd be important enough for you to mention."

"Well, I'm not your typical fairy."

That was certainly true. "No, you sure aren't."

The more time I spent with Finn, the more I liked him, though I knew I shouldn't. He was not only our bitter enemy, a Winter fairy, he was the *Prince* of Winter. That didn't seem to matter, though. No matter how hard I tried, my brain refused to stop liking him, stop enjoying his company, stop wanting to be with him. My heart swelled whenever he looked my way, and I wondered—not for the first time—if this was love.

After another season passed, we still spent all our time together when Finn was in Summer. Every thirty sundowns, he'd leave to go home for a recharge. He would be gone for four or five sundowns and then return to Summer. Back to me.

One day we snuck out of the castle, and Finn gave

me a funny look.

"Delle, come with me."

"Where?"

"It's a secret."

We flew over prairies, flower filled fields, and cascading mountains. He surprised me by taking us to the border of Winter. As a Summer fairy, I'd never been this close. There had never been a reason to go there. Why would we intentionally put ourselves in danger? The longer we stayed in the other's court, the more our glamour drained, and no one wanted to find out what happened to a fairy if they had no more magic. Plus, there was one other danger: no one wanted to know what Queen Mab would do if she caught a Summer fairy in her lands.

Finn stepped over the invisible line and crossed into Winter's territory, glowing bright blue for an instant. It was beautiful, but the idea of what we were actually doing terrified me. How could I cross that line?

He saw the concern in my face and conjured a coat for me, made of down feathers. "You'll survive the cold," he promised, so I let him take my hand and lead me across the border.

In that moment I thought I understood how Finn must have felt when he'd come to Summer. Emotions swirled through me, and while I was thrilled to experience something new, I'll admit I was scared. As he led me across the new landscape, he squeezed my fingers to boost my confidence, and he didn't object to my slow, careful pace.

Everything around me sparkled. With him beside me I admired a different beauty from what I was used to. I hadn't realized that nature had a way of making everything—the frozen trees, white frosted grass, and crystalized flowers—look special.

I tipped my face up to the sky and let snowflakes melt on my tongue. The snow tickled my skin like little pinpricks, making me giggle. Finn smiled, seeing my obvious wonder, then led me to a beautiful lake. He stepped fearlessly onto the surface, but I stopped at the edge, shaking my head. The smooth blue water seemed real enough for me to scoop up a handful to drink, but Finn promised me it was frozen solid and we wouldn't fall through. I tapped my foot against the solid barrier then tentatively placed my weight on it before adding my second foot. I cried out when I slipped, but Finn caught me in his strong arms. He helped me get to a large boulder so I could lean against it.

"Well?" he said.

I stared around me at the frosted world, amazed. "Winter is so . . . I can't think of a word that would describe it well enough. It's just—"

"Breathtaking," he suggested, looking proud. "Now we're going to do something that I know *you've* never experienced before." He bent over and touched my slippers, creating blades underneath them. I wobbled, arms outstretched for balance, but he wrapped an arm around me and led me onto the ice. "This is called skating."

It was freeing to feel the cold wind blowing against my face and skin, but I could barely stay upright. Finn was patient. He held my hand and kept his other on my waist, helping and guiding me, steering us up and down, across and around. We never tired.

Eventually the moon poked its face above the horizon, and its white glow blanketed Winter in soft light. Neither Finn nor I cared how late it was or how cold the night had become. We were content in each other's arms. When Finn finally stopped moving, my ankles wobbled on the thin slice of ice Finn had attached to my slippers, and I sailed past him. I felt the firm, safe grip of his hand on my arm, and he pulled me back against his chest. I stared up at him, caught in his eyes when he stared into mine.

Then he kissed me.

The coolness that brushed my lips traveled down my throat and into my stomach, momentarily freezing my legs to the spot. I threw my arms around his neck and kissed him so hard. We fell into a pile of soft snow he created just in time. Everything about this moment felt perfect, from the cool strength of his hands to the way the icy blue of his eyes seemed to melt when I looked up at him. After a while he lay back beside me, lying on the cold surface of the ice, and we stared into the sky, watching snowflakes dust the air.

I was falling for him just as fast as the snow fell around us.

Chapter 8

"Can you keep a secret?" Finn asked at the next sundown. We had just returned from Winter and had managed to sneak back into my room without being caught. "I want to show you something that I found when I first came to Summer."

My stomach fluttered at the idea of sharing another secret, despite my having spent hundreds of sundowns with him. When he stood like that, his muscular arm stretched out and waiting for me, I still felt a little weak in my knees.

I nodded and set my hand in his as I rose from the chaise. "Lead the way." He didn't say anything more, so I couldn't help asking, "Where are we going?"

He chuckled, and his deep voice sent a thrill racing through me. I loved hearing his warm, sultry voice, feeling his cool touch. "I'm not telling you. It's a surprise."

I adored everything about Finn. At times, when I sat alone in my room waiting for the sun to set, I thought of him. I saw flashes of his expressions in others' faces, and I often wondered what he would say about different topics. I simply couldn't stop thinking of him.

Best of all, I trusted him. I knew without any doubt

he had my best interests in mind.

But as we strolled from the castle, something nudged my senses. The hairs on the back of my neck rose. It felt like a warning, but I dismissed it, certain it was just my excitement over our secret outing.

Finn squeezed my hand. "We're almost there. It's just over that hill."

"I've never seen you this excited before," I told him. "This must be something really good."

He grinned, his eyes dancing. "In the nine seasons we've known each other, I've only wanted to share this with you." His step carried a slight bounce. "There hasn't been anyone else."

The idea of sharing his secret rushed through me and burned pleasantly in my cheeks. He tugged on my hand, and we ran over the grassy hills, darting through the shadowy trees. At last the forest ahead of us lightened, meaning we were coming to an open area. But when we burst from the trees, I was disappointed. In front of us lay an open pasture, no more, and the place was eerily silent. Even stranger, no flowers bloomed there, and not one bird chirped.

I slumped. "What's so special about this place?"

"Just wait. Watch this." Finn let go of my hand and waded into the tall grass. As he stepped, the green shoots bent under his feet, but they stood immediately at attention as he moved forward. Somehow they hadn't flattened under his weight. He turned and motioned me to follow. "Isn't this neat? Come on."

"How did you find this place?" I fanned the tops of the waist-high stalks with my hand, and they did the same as the grass shoots had done under his feet.

"I stumbled across it when I was exploring. Can you feel it?"

"Feel what?"

"Glamour is protecting something here."

I stopped staring at the non-moving grass and concentrated, circling my magic around my body. It shimmered but didn't follow any of my thoughts. I didn't understand. I should've been able to manipulate the wind and trees, or at least create some flowers. After all, we were still within Summer's borders. But nothing sparked.

"That isn't even the best part," Finn said, waving me over. "Come this way."

He led me to the center of the open space, and his dark blue wings spread behind him. I followed suit, letting my green wings open wide, then we both launched into the air. We flew high enough that we could see above the trees, and I saw the area was in the shape of a perfect triangle. Tall pines lined the outer edge and gradually gave way to the grasses. Beyond the triangle, random leaves fell from trees, water brushed the shoreline, and butterflies dotted the sky. Inside the tree line, it felt like this place was alive yet dead at the same time.

"What do you think is being protected?" I asked.

Finn's smile was contagious. "I don't know, but I thought you might like to explore it with me."

"You bet I would!"

I flew low into the trees, using all my senses to try and understand nature's strange behavior. Nothing appeared threatening, so I landed and walked the grounds, scanning for clues. In the exact center of the triangle lay a large silver boulder, and it pulsed with an energy that dwarfed my glamour. An uneasy feeling washed over me as I neared the midpoint of the triangle, but I stretched my arm toward the boulder, wanting to feel its power.

Finn touched my shoulder, pulling me from my

trance-like state. I hadn't even heard him land. "Delle?"

"Wh—What?" I shook my head, but I couldn't look away from the boulder. "I—"

"I know. I feel it, too. I think it's drawing us to it."

"But why?"

"I don't know." Finn shrugged. "Want to find out?"

"What if it's dangerous?"

He hesitated. "You're right. Don't touch it. You stay back and see what happens when I do it."

But what if I was right? What if it was a threat? How could I allow Finn to just march in there and be brave enough for both of us? On the other hand, what if something happened and he needed me to help him? If I kept away from the strange power, maybe I could be of some use after all. I nodded reluctantly, but when I turned away Finn grabbed my hand and pulled me back.

"Delle."

Our eyes met and held. I never wanted to move from that place, that moment. Finn swallowed, looking unusually nervous. He was usually so confident, and for some reason I found that vulnerable side of him to be very sweet.

"Before I go," he said, "I just want to say something. You know, just in case something . . . *does* happen." The intensity of his blue eyes was electric. "I want you to know that I have really enjoyed our time together. I never thought someone like you could . . . you know . . . could be with someone like me, and . . ." He cleared his throat and raked his hand through his black hair. "I—"

I rolled to my tiptoes and kissed his cool lips. "I love you, too, Finn. And you know me well enough to know I'd never let you do anything like this without me." I kissed him again. "Nothing bad is going to happen as long as we're together."

"You're sure?"

"I'm sure."

"It might not be safe, you know. There's so much power here—"

"Finn. I understand. Let's do this thing." I grabbed his hand, and we both touched the stone at the same time.

Darkness enveloped us, and I lost all sense of direction, free falling into the unknown. I tried to scream for Finn, but no sound came from my mouth. I fumbled for his hand, but my fingers couldn't find it. My stomach landed in my throat, and a wave of intense heat surrounded me. A second later, a hint of lilies, salt, and sweet fruits filled my nostrils. Light pooled below me, and I landed with a thud on soft white sand, my breath shoved from my lungs. I fought to regain my breath and adjust my vision to the sudden brightness of the sun. When I turned to examine my surroundings, Finn's body dropped from the sky and landed flat on the ground.

"Finn!" I scrambled over to him, and my hands went to his face. "Are you hurt?"

"Mmm. Where are we?"

I tried to roll him over with no success. He was as heavy as an ice brick. "I have no idea."

He lifted his head then laid it back into the damp sand with a soft groan. "Delle, are you hurt?"

"No."

He sniffed then grimaced. "What is that awful stench?"

I sniffed as well but shook my head. "I don't smell anything bad." He closed his eyes, still looking pained by the smell in the air that I couldn't sense. I looked around, wanting to figure out where we'd ended up. A sandy beach stretched for miles around us. I'd never seen anything like it in the city of Aestas or in Fairyland.

"Oh, Finn! Look at the water! It's *aqua*. That's not

the color of water in Summer."

Finn grunted. "Okay," he said, rising slowly. "I'm up."

"You *are* hurt!" I helped him stand while trying to determine what was injured. "Tell me what hurts. You don't have to play macho with me."

"I'm fine," he assured me. "It's just that the heat is draining my glamour. It's even hotter here than it is in your territory." He wiped his brow and squinted into the distance. "So that means we aren't in Summer. Maybe we're not even in Fairyland anymore. We'd better do some investigating, find out what's going on."

I wrapped one arm around Finn's waist and picked a direction. He leaned against me as we walked along the unfamiliar shore. The scorching sun beat down on us, and though I didn't mind it, I could only imagine what this was doing to Finn. He'd barely survived in Summer until the Winter guard had come to recharge him. I had to find a way to shield him from the temperature.

"How are we going to get back to Fairyland?" I asked.

Finn grabbed the side of his head, obviously suffering. "I'm working on that one."

A row of slender, tall trees stretched before us, their bright green fronds rustling. Curious groups of green ovals clustered at the junctions where the dark tree trunks met the leaves.

"What do you think those are?" I wondered out loud.

"I don't know, but they stink. Can't you smell that?" By this point, he looked not only weak but physically ill. "I think I'm going to be sick."

"You can smell them from here?" I stopped and looked around, but we were all alone. The only things following us were our footsteps, cutting a path through the pristine white sand. "Do you think our glamour works here?" I asked, staring up at the green ovals. "Maybe I could go get one and see what it is."

He nodded. "Try it."

I closed my eyes, imagining I was sitting in one of the trees. A warm glow surrounded me, and I felt the tree's hard bark materialize under my hand. When I opened my eyes, the front of my body was pressed on top of flat, spiked leaves. They hung like umbrellas over what looked like giant green pearls.

I grinned down at Finn and reached for one of the green balls. "Catch this when it falls."

"Careful," he said.

I twisted, balancing my legs on separate branches. A green ball grazed my fingertips, but I pulled back when the branch made a *cracking* sound.

"I think you'd better hurry," Finn said. "It doesn't look like the branch is going to support your weight."

I glared at him. "Are you saying I'm fat?"

"No!" His hands shot upward like he was defending himself. "I just heard the—"

"Choose your next words carefully," I warned, "because—"

The branch gave way, and I plunged toward the ground.

"Delle!" I heard, then everything went black.

Chapter 9

Sand shifted beneath my body, but my head was safely nestled in Finn's lap. His cool fingers stroked my hair as consciousness returned, and I mentally cringed, recalling what had happened. I had gotten upset over nothing, and was so busy arguing I hadn't heard the branch snap in half. Fortunately, before I dropped, I'd managed to rip one of the green balls off the branch.

"I have it," I muttered, startling him. He blinked down at me as I patted my sides, looking for the thing, but found nothing. "Or at least I thought I did."

Now that my thinking was more clear, I noticed his face had turned an even darker gray, and his body was colder than it should have been.

He pointed over his shoulder with his thumb. "I put it over there for safe keeping until you woke up." He frowned, clearly not interested in the green prize. He had other things on his mind. "Delle, don't be that reckless again," he said quietly. The hand that had been stroking my hair moved to my face, where it caressed my cheek. "When you fell, I thought . . . well, I was afraid that you were . . . you know."

"How long have I been out?" I rolled my head to the side and saw the last rays of sun kissing the water. I'd been unconscious for a while then. I looked back up at Finn with concern. "We should get you out of the sun. I don't think you're doing well."

He didn't seem to hear me. "You fell so hard, and then you didn't move. I didn't know if you'd be all right, and . . ." He laid his hand against my cheek, so cold against my warm skin. His eyes were bluer than the sea. "I love you, Delle," he said quietly. A brief, self-conscious smile crossed his face. "There. I said it."

My heart soared, and I giggled. "What did you say? I didn't quite catch it."

"You heard me."

"Maybe, but I think you need to say it again."

He held my face in his palm, and his thumb brushed tenderly over my lips. "I love you, Sidelle."

We stared into each other's eyes until the sun disappeared under the horizon, casting brilliant reds and oranges across the sky. It was beautiful, but I couldn't help being distracted. We needed a plan. That included building a shelter, figuring out where we were, and maybe even getting home.

"So. How do you propose we get back to Fairyland?"

He sighed. "I was thinking about that while you were unconscious," he said, frowning slightly. "I didn't want to wander too far in case you woke up. I figure you'd have been scared if I wasn't there."

"You know," I said, sitting up and tucking my feet under me, "you can be sweet when you're not calling me fat."

He looked at me quickly, his expression horrified. "But I didn't—"

"I know," I admitted, raising my hand to stop him. "I'm teasing. Besides, it was my idea to be up in the tree in the first place." Curious, I reached for the green ball lying in the sand beside me and shook it. Nothing rattled inside, so I knocked on the outside. Digging my fingers in, I tried to pry off some of the green layer, but it was stubborn.

Eventually I was able to peel away a small chunk, and I discovered a brown husk inside. "What do you think this is?"

He grimaced again. "Not edible, if you ask me. It reeks."

"It's definitely not a grape. Here." I tossed it to him. "See if you can pry off the hairy layer."

Frowning with concentration, Finn easily ripped off what remained of the outer coat, but he couldn't get any deeper. "I think I need something sharp." He shook his head. "I don't understand why you're so fascinated with this."

I shrugged. "I don't know. I've never seen anything like it before, so I'm curious. That's all." Nearby I spotted a rock pile. "Look over there. See if you can smash it against one of the edges."

"Maybe I should find or make us a shelter," he grumbled.

"You can do that *after* you get this thing open. When the sun comes up, we can explore and figure out how to get home."

Finn's steps faltered as he walked away, but he refused to ask for help. I shook my head and sighed, wondering at his stubborn male pride. Getting to my feet, I brushed off my sandy dress and noticed a group of low lying branches that could provide shade. I gathered armfuls of large leaves from the overgrown foliage and arranged them by length. As I focused my thoughts my glamour flared, and with my magic I created a nice little hut.

I stepped back to admire my work then stopped, the

hair standing up on the back of my neck. I was being watched. I spun around in time to see a pair of glowing eyes blink at me before they melted back into the shadows. My pulse raced at the unexpected encounter. In the whole time we had been here, I had taken for granted that we were alone. I'd never thought about wild animals or other beings.

"Um, Finn?" I whispered as loudly as I could. "You need to come here." I took a step backward, away from the presence in the trees. "There's something—or someone—here with us."

Finn didn't reply, so I assumed he hadn't heard me. He was still hunched over the rock pile, trying to break open the ball, and I was suddenly alarmed by his appearance. Sweat dripped from his wilting body, and his breathing seemed labored. He obviously needed to rest, but I knew he wouldn't listen to that suggestion. Then his legs buckled, and his lower body splashed into the water.

Forgetting all about the threat in the shadows, I ran over and rolled him onto his back. "Finnegan!" He didn't move. "Oh, fairy! Wake up!"

I dragged him out of the water and carefully brushed wet sand from his face, blinking hard to keep from crying. My palm pressed against his chest, over his heart, and I felt it beat, though the rhythm was sporadic. His body was ashen, and small icicles hung in his hair. All I could think was that if he were warm, he would heal. If he were like me, he'd be all right. I could think of no other options, so I called for my glamour, needing it more than I'd ever needed it before. I had no idea if it would on a Winter fairy, but I had to try.

Green magic swirled around me, and I directed all of it to my hand. My palm grew warm and the heat built until it reached a smoldering temperature. I pressed it against Finn's frozen chest and forced my essence into him. His body began to warm from the inside, then a blast of coldness shot back into my hand and shoved me backward. I scrambled back to him, but he laid still. Forcing Summer into him hadn't work.

"Finn! Please!" I cried, tears streaming down my cheeks. "Come back to me!"

In the next instant, Finn's upper body convulsed and shot up so he was sitting. "What were you saying?"

I stared at him, speechless, then I hugged him as tightly as I could. My tears came from joy this time. "Oh my fairy! You're not dead!"

He patted his legs and arms then shook his head. "Nope. Now what were you saying before?"

"Don't change the subject," I scolded. "Are you really okay?"

"Yes." He rubbed his chest. "Come on, Delle."

"There was something in the tree line," I told him, pointing behind me.

"Is that all?" He shrugged. "You can take care of it, whatever it is. I'm surprised at you. I didn't think you would be scared of a little animal. Wherever we are, I'm sure they don't have things as big as Dragons."

I glared. "Finn. I'm serious. We need to check it out. Something is not right."

"So *now* you need me to protect you?" he asked, one eyebrow lifted.

"No. I just . . ." I inhaled then let it out. "Just go take a look. Please?"

"First you want me to do this," he muttered. "Then you want me to do that. Jeez, Delle. Make up your mind." As he rose from the ground, a smile grew on his face. "You're getting bossy in your old age."

I gasped. "First I'm fat, and now I'm old?" I stood, hands on my hips. "You are treading on very thin ice,

Finnegan."

"I like living on the edge." Finn patted my arm as he passed. "Here. I got it open," he said, handing me the pieces of the ball. He looked at the shelter I'd built, and I saw approval in his blue eyes. "Nice shack. You did good, my love. We can call it the love shack."

I rolled my eyes, but my attention was drawn back to the mystery item. I peered inside the halves of the ball and frowned at the white, watery substance within. I inhaled a sweet aroma, so I dipped a tentative finger into the creamy substance. A drop stuck to the tip of my nail, and I licked it off. It tasted like bitter water.

"That is where I saw it," I told Finn, pointing into the trees again.

He stopped where I had seen the eyes, and I heard him chuckle as he stepped through the canopy of branches and into the wooded area.

The full moon appeared high in the sky, lighting the mysterious white liquid. I tasted it again, curious, then I gazed out at the water. The reflection of the moon on the ripples was mesmerizing, distracting me momentarily from the question of where we were. A few seconds later, I returned my gaze to the spot where I'd last seen Finn, wondering what was going on. I listened for sounds, but didn't hear anything, which was strange. I should have at least heard footsteps. Glamour coursed through my fingers, and I shot an illuminating ball of Fairy Light into the darkness a few feet ahead of me.

A twig snapped and something rustled nearby, coming closer. I glanced around, looking for a weapon of some kind, but the approaching noise distracted me. Finally, I grabbed a small tree, used my glamour to reshape it into a sword, then I pointed it to the opening of the woods.

"Sidelle!" Finn's voice floated from the woods.

"Finn?" I screamed back. "Are you okay? What's happening?"

"Delle!" he shouted, sounding terrified. "Run! Get out of here!"

What could scare him this badly? My heart raced, and I held my makeshift sword higher. "I'm not leaving you!"

"Run, Delle, now!" The tone of his voice frightened me nearly as much as the unknown threat that grew around us. I became aware of a heavy drumming on the ground, as if a herd of animals was coming hard and fast, and all the hair on my arms stood on end. "I'm right behind you," he yelled. "I'll find you. I promise."

That was something I couldn't do. I unfurled my wings, ready for anything. "No! I won't leave you."

For an instant the whole place was lit by lightning, though I hadn't seen a cloud in the sky. Finn's outline became visible just beyond the tree line. Suddenly the sand and water were pelted by rain, and a chorus of howls erupted into the night. The pounding under my feet grew louder, shaking the ground, and the branches at the entrance of the woods shook as something ran through them. Whatever chased Finn was hot on his heels.

My wings expanded and I focused, harnessing the atmosphere's energy, preparing to direct it at Finn's pursuers. As he neared the tree line, I started running toward him.

"No!" he screamed, frantically waving his arms. "Go back to the water! They're coming!"

I pulled my glamour around me, preparing to flash to the sandy edge, but I waited stubbornly for Finn. He passed under the archway made by the trees boughs, his fingers touched my arm, then darkness blanketed us again.

Chapter 10

We were dumped into a small lake, and I swallowed a mouthful of water, but a multitude of tiny hands pushed me to the surface. I gulped air when I cleared the top, then coughed out the water. When I opened my eyes, bright pairs of multi-colored eyes stared back.

"Thank you," I said.

"You're very welcome, my Lady," one of the Water sprites said. "It's an honor to assist you."

I glanced around, worried. "Do you know where my companion is? He's wearing a blue—"

The speaker shook her head. "We do not help Winter."

"I need to find him." I waved my hand over my hair, and the water droplets disappeared from my bangs. I stared at the little sprite, confused. "Am I back in Fairyland?"

"Did you leave?" another one asked.

It *couldn't* have been a dream. Everything had felt so real: the warm sun on my face, the salty air, and the strange, cerulean water. I had witnessed a sunset painted with a palette of colors we didn't have here. Not only that, but everything about Finn had changed, from the pasty gray of his skin to the way it seemed the sun sucked his life force with every breath.

"Sidelle?"

His voice came from behind me, and I spun to see him. He lay on the shore, his body partially submerged in the murky water.

"Finn! I'm here!" I ran to his side. "Are you okay?"

He groaned. "I've been better. Swimming is not fun. What about you? Are you hurt?"

"No." I sat beside him. "But you'll be glad to know we're back in Fairyland. Do me a favor? Tell me that what just happened, really happened."

"What?"

I tilted my head toward the sprites. "When I asked if I was in Fairyland, they looked at me like I had two heads. As if they couldn't understand why I'd asked that. So I started to wonder . . ."

"If you'd dreamed it?" He shook his head. "Nope. It was very strange but very real." He glanced around. "This is our pond."

"It is!" I recognized the familiar pathway, the trees, and the distinct hum of the land. "But how did we get here?"

"I think we went through a portal of some kind." Finn stood then stretched. "And that stone in the field must have been one, too, since it brought us into the Ordinaries' world." He took a few steps then faltered.

I rushed to his side. "Really? That's where we were?"

"Yes. I think we were in the human's realm."

The idea fascinated me. How easy to forget the danger when there was so much to discover! He leaned against me for support, though I thought he was looking a little better.

"Do you think that will always happen if you go back?"

He cocked his head. "What are you talking about?"

"The heat, I mean. It was like you were being drained of your energy."

"I was fine," he grumbled, standing a little taller.

"Nope. Sorry. I saw what you looked like. It wasn't right."

"I was fine," he insisted.

I shrugged. "Whatever. You keep telling yourself that, but I know the truth. Now come on. We need to go back to Aestas Castle. I'm not sure how long I have been gone. My father is probably about to send out the troops." My body shimmered, creating new, dry clothes and cleaning my face.

"Delle?" Finn reached for my hand. "I'm glad you were there with me, but I can't go back to your castle. I need to go to my home to recharge." His smile was soft. "Don't worry. I promise I'll be back for you soon." With that, he vanished.

A split second later I materialized in my room, wanting some time to myself so I could reflect on my experience. I craved the comfort of my bed and sighed as I curled under the duvet. With Finn back in Winter, his home, a small part of my heart ached.

Just then Brea pounced on me, squashing my solitude. "The king's looking for you."

I blinked at her, curious. "How long has he been looking?"

She shrugged. "He just asked me to find you. You should go see him."

Time had apparently stretched while we were on the beach. Our time there had felt like hours, but from what I could tell, it had only been moments. I walked down the hallways toward the throne room, wondering what Father wanted. By now he probably knew the Winter fairy was missing, but I couldn't tell him what had happened between Finn and me. Should I tell him about the strange experience we'd had on the beach? I didn't understand any of it, and the odd passage of time baffled me.

I took a deep breath and pushed open the double oak doors that led into the throne room.

"Sidelle!" King Oberon said, welcoming me. A frown touched his brow. "Have you seen that Prince? He's missing, you know. Did he steal you away?"

"Father. I'm fine," I assured him. "I—"

"Were you fairynapped by that Prince?" His eyes narrowed with rage. "When I get my hands around his scrawny little neck, I'm going to—"

"Father, no!" I waved my hands. "Finnegan didn't do anything wrong. Besides, he's back in Winter now."

"Wait." He stepped back, assessing me. "There's something different about you. You've been ..." He inhaled, and his fingers lifted my chin so he could inspect me more closely. "You've been to the mortal's world, haven't you? How?"

What a relief. I wouldn't have to explain all of it to him. "I didn't go there on purpose. I didn't even know where I was. I . . .." My jaw dropped open. "How do you even know I was there? Have *you* been there?"

He lifted his chin. "This is not about me. This is about you." He nodded. "I can see it and smell it on you. You . . . ate something while you were there."

My hand cupped my mouth.

"It smells like . . ." He inhaled. "Coconut." He squinted at me again. "And there is something else different about you, too. I'll figure it out."

"Is that what it was? A coconut? It tasted strange."

"What else did you see?"

"Nothing. It was a white sandy beach with the most pristine turquoise water. Behind that there was a wooded area, but I didn't actually get a chance to explore."

"You didn't get hurt while you were there?"

I smiled, putting him at ease. "No. I'm fine. I fell out of the tree when I was getting the coconut, but everything else was good. Why? Can I really get injured there?"

"Not by humans or their animals, but you do have to watch how you use your glamour. You can't let them see it. They'll know you are different and won't understand why. It's not safe for Eternals there." He embraced me again. "I'm glad you're okay, Sidelle." He held up one finger. "But you are never to go near the Porta Stone again."

Twenty sundowns passed after our adventure into the world of the Ordinaries, and I checked all our usual spots in the forest, but Finn didn't return. Sometimes I waited there until the next sunrise, but he never came. I wanted to tell him what I'd learned about the portal, ask him how he felt now that he was back in his own court.

Most of all, I wanted to see him. I felt a little empty without him around.

But he never came to me. Eventually I conceded that he had probably gone back to his home and forgotten all about his promise to return.

By the fortieth day, I grew concerned. Finn had never been away this long. Maybe he just couldn't get away, but I couldn't help worrying. Since I'd never been to Winter, I didn't know how Queen Mab ran her court. Maybe he wasn't allowed to just up and leave whenever he wanted to. He might have obligations that even I didn't know about.

Or . . . he might have been scared off since we'd said

those three little words to each other. What if that was it? No. He wouldn't be like that, would he?

By the sixtieth sundown, I'd given up. I quit going to our special places; I stopped hoping.

Father came out and sat next to me in the garden one day. He took my hand. "Sidelle?" he said. "You've been lethargic for a while lately. I think I know something that will cheer you up."

"I'm fine," I said.

"I've decided," he announced quietly, "that I would like you to be the Summer Representative at the next Change of the Seasons Ceremony. It's a great privi—"

"I'm honored." Really I was, but my voice sounded monotone. "When is it again?"

He clucked his tongue at me. "Sidelle," he said, disappointed. "Twelve sundowns from now."

"Okay. Thank you for the opportunity, Father. I have wanted to do more with my existence lately, and now you've given me a way to do that."

"Ah. What to do with our existence," he said, smiling wistfully. "One of life's many questions. This will be perfect then."

I hung my head. I couldn't believe what I was about to say. "I've been thinking about what you once told me."

He sat up, eager to hear which of his words had made an impression on me. "And that is?"

"I think I should get more friends. Get out there and show Fairyland that I'm not just a princess, but someone who can lead, someone who can be a role model that this court can be proud of."

"Oh?" He sagged just a little. "Well, that's great, of course. I had hoped you'd changed your mind on that *other* matter." He squeezed my hand. "But I'll take this little victory. Which lucky Fairies do you wish to add to your inner circle?"

"About that." I turned away from him. "I would like to travel the world and get to know what else is out there. I want to have experiences of my own." I took a deep breath for courage. "I would like your blessing to go back to the human—"

"Absolutely not!" He stood and fisted his hands. "You are too young and too inexperienced. I forbid it."

"But—"

"But nothing. I will not have this conversation with you again." He started to walk away, then stopped and looked back at me. His gaze was soft again. "And Sidelle? Try to remember I'm proud of you—even though you love to torment me.

Chapter 11

Two sundowns before the next season change, I prepared for the scepter exchange at the altar, and my mind wandered back to Finn. My body thrummed with anticipation. Would I see him there? Possibly. I paced my large bedroom and kept a running commentary going through my head. It hurt that he had blown me off, but I still needed to know what had happened. Neither of us could deny there had been something special between us. I simply couldn't understand why he'd dropped me. I needed to hear an explanation. He owed me that much.

I was startled by a knock on my door. "Yes?" I asked. "Enter."

"So it's true?" Brea skipped across the threshold. "I can't believe he's sending you into the frozen nest! Doesn't he realize what's he's doing to you?"

She knew how I was both dreading and looking forward to this big moment. "It's over, Brea. I just have to accept that." I flattened my emerald green skirt and removed the wrinkles with a wave of my hand. "He didn't even give me a reason. He told me he loved me then bailed. He's a jerk, and I don't ever want to think about him again."

"So you're not planning to see him when you get there?" Brea flopped onto my bed. "Because if you—"

"I'm sure he'll have to attend the festivities since he's a prince. If I do see him, I'm going to turn my back and keep walking." I twirled, letting my gown spin like prairie grass in the wind.

"Good." She grinned. "Think you'll actually see him?"

I scowled. "If he knows what's good for him, he won't come near me." I clenched my hands then relaxed them and combed my fingers through my long black hair. Each strand found its place and tied itself into a neat braid which spiraled on top of my head.

Brea patted my back sympathetically. "Be strong, Sid. Don't let him back into your life. After everything he put you though this last season, he doesn't deserve you." She waved her hand across my golden crown and tiny bright pink flowers appeared.

I hugged her tight, grateful for her kind words. "Thanks, Brea."

"For what?"

"For being my friend."

"Aw, shucks." She punched my shoulder. "Now stop being so emotional. You need to bury those feelings. Show all of Winter that you're strong."

The Summer procession assembled outside the Aestas Castle, and we journeyed the long road to Winter. I sat atop my pet dragon Betsy in the last golden howdah, which carried the season's offerings: an array of wild flowers, dried fruits, and the pale but glowing yellow scepter. We moved forward at a snail's pace, and Betsy tossed her head, snorting her frustration. She loved to run, but I held her back. The pomp and circumstance couldn't be rushed. The longer we held the scepter, the longer Summer lasted. That meant we didn't need to use glamour to travel through the lands for the exchange.

Two sundowns later, when our caravan entered Winter's borders, I saw snowcapped mountains, icicles, and massive frozen lakes. It was the first time I'd gone far enough into Winter that I could see those, though Finn had shown me what he could. Seeing the landscape now created a rush of memories, and I recalled the first time he'd kissed me. The moment had been magical, just like the atmosphere around me. That kiss felt like it had happened lifetimes ago. I shook my head and cleared my thoughts. There was no point in reminiscing about times that didn't matter anymore. I needed to focus on the exchange.

Aesculus Castle nestled between a snow-covered mountain and a bottomless cliff. A frosty mist blanketed the land, making it impossible to see more than a few inches ahead. We traveled along a strip of ice, since it was the only road to get to the castle. The narrow pathway was suspended high above the canyon, which separated the frozen tundra from the city limits. A few of the walking Summer fairies slipped on the ice, but Betsy's large claws gripped the road.

I couldn't understand how Fairies could live in such a cold place. My castle was made from stone, and these frozen walls glistened in ice. An enormous gate towered in front of the procession, carved from a three-foot thick block of ice. My companions glanced around, nervous, but I sat ramrod straight, trying to look like royalty. I'm not sure I entirely succeeded, though. No matter how hard I tried to appear nonchalant, my eyes kept wandering, wanting to take it all in.

The parade of my kin left a trail of warmth in their

wake. I worried we would melt the bridge, then I reminded myself that this procession took place once a season, and nothing bad had happened yet. Frost-covered trees lined the corridor when the gates opened, their branches draped in icicles, looking like a shiny weeping willow. A hint of rain lingered in the air, but I couldn't figure out if it came from us or from Winter. After all, ice was only frozen water.

As we moved farther into the hall, Winter fairies began to appear. Some courageous ones tossed ice shards toward us or dared to trip a convoy member, but for the most part they left us alone. Loud, strange music floated down to the procession, its notes coming from unfamiliar instruments, indicating that Winter's festivities had started. I wondered briefly if their parties were anything like ours, with the rich foods, the drinking and dancing into the next sundown.

A shadow moved in an adjacent alcove, reminding me of . . .

My body shivered involuntarily, and I squashed the thought of Finn. I shook my head, clearing my thoughts, and was distracted by a giggle then the flash of a blue scabbard. Two bodies were trying to hide in that small space, and I caught glimpses of a navy skirt. I also heard a familiar male chuckle.

"Welcome to Aesculus Castle!" A female voice bounced and echoed off the walls, capturing my attention. "You are late, and this will not go unnoticed. When you return to Summer, tell your King that I'll hold the scepter longer next time. See if that will teach you to waste my night."

A tall woman emerged from behind an ice wall, her beautiful black hair flowing gracefully behind her and past her tiny waist. Her gown was an intricately embellished blue, the color reminiscent of a glacier.

"The exchange must happen when the land dictates it," she continued. "And She has spoken. Now you must hurry to the altar." She adjusted her gem-encrusted crown.

I was not impressed. Just because she spoke in such a manner, did not mean I was going to bend to her will. As a member of the Summer court, I would not be bullied. She might be the Queen of this land, but she didn't hold power over me or my brethren.

I stared her down. "We will arrive when we are good and ready," I informed her. "If your subjects hadn't badgered us at the gate, we would have been in the courtyard sooner."

Her eyes flashed. "How dare you speak to me with such disrespect?" Her large, dark blue wings appeared, and she hovered near my carriage. "Who do you think you are, little Fairy?" She drew herself up to be as large as she could, trying to impress us all. "I am Queen Mab of the Winter Court, and I demand respect! You are just the Summer rep."

I lifted my head high, and my gaze held hers. "I am not of your court. I do not bow to you or your demands. As a Lady of Summer, you would be wise to speak to me as my title demands." She was a glorious adversary, but I didn't blink. "Now please lead me to the altar so we may do the exchange."

"You will speak to me with respect, as *my* title is higher than yours." Her eyes narrowed and she bent toward me with a wicked smile. "I will remember this, *Lady,* and I have a very long memory. It would be wise of you to consider that."

She waved the procession forward, and my travel companions stopped at the grand ballroom, but I continued through the outer courtyard and to the back of the castle. The backdrop was spectacular: snowcapped mountains and swirling crystals danced on the air, and a frozen lake stretched to the horizon.

A frozen gazebo stood before me, surrounding a slab of solid ice at least ten inches thick. This was the altar.

"I see my representative is also late," the Queen said, looking annoyed. "He seems to do that a lot lately."

I kept my face averted, preferring to watch the snowfall. I was mesmerized by Winter's cold, silent heartbeat. A shadow moved by the altar, and I squinted through the unique flakes. I could see the outline of . . .

No. It couldn't be.

"I will go then," Queen Mab said, sounding amused. "I think you two may have some catching up to do, yes?" She turned and disappeared, but her cackle lingered on the wind.

I walked reluctantly toward the altar, having no idea what to say. I decided to let him speak first, since he was the one who had broken his promise.

Finn turned toward me, but his head remained bowed. "I'm sorry, Delle," he said quietly. "I couldn't meet you after . . . well, you know."

My eyes traveled up his familiar muscular body, his silky black hair, and stopped at his piercing blue eyes. Emotions chewed at my heart, encouraged by images of the countless late nights we'd spent talking and getting to know each other, our first kiss, the adventures we'd shared, and the three words we'd spoken to each other.

My eyes watered, and I took a step away from him. Then I remembered I was angry. This was my chance to finally get some answers. My body hummed, and my wings sprung out behind me. Like Brea had said, I needed to stay strong.

But seeing him again and recognizing the familiar posture, the confidence in his gait, I faltered. The sound of his laughter came back to me, and tears leaked down my cheeks. He'd hurt me before, but it was more than that. I'd known it was him in that alcove with another fairy—doing who knows what.

"I did try a couple of times," he said, "but Mab blocked me."

"I really don't want to hear it." I wiped my face with the back of my hand. "We have a job to do, so let's just forget about the past and focus."

"Delle. I owe you—"

I shook my head. "Don't." My voice cracked. "Don't call me that."

"Mab found out where I had spent all my time and prevented me from returning to Summer," Finn continued. "When she figured I was sneaking out to be with you, she blew her crown right off her head." He shook his head and reached for me, but I stepped away from his arms. "Please believe me, Delle. I really wanted to see you again, but she threatened to freeze me solid. I couldn't—"

"What do you want me to say? I don't care."

The sun glistened then pulsed, telling us we didn't have long before the ceremony at the altar must be completed. "Finn, just say your part so I can go home."

He blinked sadly at me then cleared his throat. "This isn't over, Delle."

Without a word, I presented him with the two-foot silver scepter. He accepted the staff's end, and we both placed it on the ice altar. The center orb glowed white, and every now and then it pulsed a soft yellow.

"Each snowflake is like the heart of Earth's memories," Finn recited. "They fall to cover her body in a white blanket. Quietness fills the frosty air. The stillness of Winter's shadow makes way for a new season. Change brought to bring new life."

My turn. Tradition required us to hold each other's

gaze as we spoke, but it was so difficult to stare at him without crying. I took a deep breath, bolstering myself.

"Snow and ice will coat the pine tree's bough," I said, removing my hand from the scepter. "The birds won't sing their melodic song. Summer remains but must leave. Summer must resign. Winter, I ask that you wake from under your wintry cover. You have waited long enough."

Finally, I looked away from him and stared instead at the scepter. As far as I knew, both parts had been said correctly, unlike at the exchange when I'd met Finn so long before. We waited to find out if we'd done it right then sighed with relief as the scepter pulsed to a radiant blue.

Chapter 12

On the sundown after the exchange, I fled to the safety of the Summer gardens and tried desperately to keep my mind from thoughts of Finn. I pulled out my parchment and quills, relaxing while I drew scene after familiar scene of prairies, unfrozen lakes, and live forests.

When I was done, I set my artwork aside and considered going to sleep on the soft green grass. Instead, I was startled awake by an unexpected ray of intense light, which created a perfect white circle on the ground next to me. A tall angel appeared within the circle, dressed in a deep blue, gauzy robe. His feet were strapped into gold sandals. With his magnificent gray wings extended, he hovered in the air around me, surrounded by the light. Eventually he floated down to where I sat.

I had seen angels in Fairyland before, but this one was different. His feathers pulsed with a power that made me flinch.

"Sidelle." He spoke with confidence. "Please take me to your father."

I nodded but was frozen in place, staring at him. Eventually he pointed toward the castle, prompting me to stand. I collected my drawings and couldn't help pausing, studying the last one I'd drawn, then I made them all disappear. Seeing that I was ready, the angel flapped his wings, tucked them into his back, and walked beside me.

"I haven't been here in a long while." He turned his head thoughtfully. "Things don't change."

"How do you know my name?" I asked. "I've never seen you before."

"I know a great deal about you." He looked into my eyes, but I couldn't read his meaning. "More than you know."

My stomach fluttered, and he placed his hand on my shoulder. His palm lit with a soft yellow light, warm against my skin. "You are sad," he said, "but that will pass. As I said before, things don't change—but Beings do."

He moved his hand away, and in its place there remained a shimmering green tattoo, a lily encased in a beautiful pair of green, iridescent wings. I ran my finger across it then looked up questioningly at the angel.

"It will protect you," he explained.

I was confused. "I don't need protection."

His smile was gentle. "Maybe not at this precise moment, but someday you might." He laid his hand on my forearm. "Now you are marked as one of His followers."

I didn't know what or who he was talking about, but I filed my questions into the back of my mind. There was no time for them now, since we were approaching the throne room doors. When they opened, King Oberon stood in his most colorful blue and green robes.

"Michael," Oberon exclaimed happily, opening his arms for an embrace. "Welcome to Aestas."

I stared at him, then at the angel, stunned. Did he mean the *Archangel Michael?*

Yes, child, I heard in my mind. *One and the same.*

I stood motionless, barely able to think. Father, on the other hand, seemed entirely at ease with him.

"What brings you to Fairyland?" Oberon asked as they walked deeper into the castle, leaving me behind.

"May I speak openly?" I heard Michael ask.

"Of course," Father replied, their voices fading away into the distance.

I knew where Oberon would take the angel, so I reappeared behind the massive oak that grew on the north side of the king's private courtyard, hoping I hadn't missed too much of their conversation.

"I see," Oberon said, nodding sagely as they walked into the courtyard. "I will do the same as the angels."

Apparently I had missed it. I hoped Father would be in a sharing mood after.

"Good," Michael said. "I hoped you would. I don't know how long it will be."

"It will be however long it needs to be," Father replied, then he stood. "I will assemble a team by nightfall. Never fear, Michael. We will prevail, my brother."

Michael rose and snapped his wings outward. He tilted his head toward where I thought I was well hidden, winked, then disappeared. I wasn't overly surprised. It only made sense that it would be impossible to hide from an angel who could speak in my mind.

I peeked out from behind the tree. "Father? Assemble for what?"

"You shouldn't have been listening."

I hung my head. "I know. I couldn't help it."

He reached for me, so I walked toward him. "You have been sad lately." He kissed my forehead and pulled me close. "You gave a piece of your soul to that Winter Prince when you brought him back from the brink of death on the beach in the Ordinaries' world." I looked up, stunned that he knew all that. He nodded sadly. "Oh, yes. I know about it. But Sidelle, fairies can die by infusing too much of ones' essence into another. The amount you gave him has made you a fairy of both Summer and Winter. It has changed your status in both courts."

He held me out at arms' length, his hands on my shoulders, his expression serious. "What you did, Sidelle, has changed the seasons. You will now lead into the Summer season and he will lead into the Winter season." He frowned sympathetically. "For both of those reasons, I wish I could make your heart heal."

I hung my head. "I'm told it will pass."

"It does, but it will take a while." He hesitated. "I think you should leave Fairyland for a while."

What? I blinked at him, confused, but to my utter surprise, my overly protective father appeared to be completely serious. "Come, let's go for a walk outside of the castle," he said, taking my hand. In a second we appeared on the edge of the Wild Forest, near the path that led to my hidden spot. Maybe it wasn't quite as secret as I'd thought. "In response to your earlier question about my conversation with Michael, I will be deploying a team of fairies to search for The Redeemer."

"Who's that?"

"The angel said there will be a human girl born who will save the world from Armageddon. That's the Prophesy."

"What does it say, exactly?"

He cleared his throat and looked straight ahead, concentrating on the words. "It says,

Glory!
Babe born.
First and last.

Heaven and unto Earth;
Receives the highest in jubilation.
Enlightens will unite; they shall band.
Triumph be if darkness is driven back.
Help found who love, the world will stand."

For a moment I couldn't speak. He was speaking about a tremendous event, and the magnitude of it left me slightly bewildered. "When will she be born?" I eventually asked.

He looked into the sky and smiled sadly. "That is the golden question."

I paced slowly, letting the words of the Prophesy roll around in my mind. "So if no one knows who she is, how are the Eternals going to find her?"

"I would speculate the earth will somehow let us know." He touched the bark of an old maple tree, and a face appeared, followed by the giggle of a tree Nymph.

Since he didn't seem to have many more answers, I went back to his original suggestion. The one that had practically knocked me over with surprise. Were the two connected? "Tell me, Father, how long will I be gone? And where am I going?"

He smiled to himself. "Until you find her. You're going to the Ordinaries' world," he said, gathering fallen tree limbs together and weaving the branches into an archway. He stood by it then finally looked at me, making sure I understood the importance of this mission. "You will be the lead Summer fairy. You must gather information and report back to me every few human years."

I nodded. My trepidation was quickly being overshadowed by anticipation of the adventure. "I can come home when I want?"

"Oh, yes. Whenever you want or need to. I am not

banishing you." Oberon waved his hand over the wooden arch until the inside shimmered and opened, revealing an ancient castle set on top of a hill, surrounded by rolling pastures. "I just thought you wouldn't want to be around here all the time, where you are constantly reminded of him."

I nodded, thinking hard, then I stepped toward the arch. This was my chance for change. I would get away, explore, and re-invent myself. "I will go and do what you ask of me, Father," I told him. "And I declare my oath to find her."

I stepped through the portal.

PART II

Chapter 13

Year Eleven Hundred

When I stepped from the archway, my feet landed in soft mud. At least, I hoped that's what it was, not some animal—*don't even think it*. I kept myself invisible until I could figure out where I was, and my eyes scanned the area. A path that had seen better days stretched out in front of me, both sides lined by trees. In the distance on the left, a stone castle stood on the hill, complete with round gray turrets. I decided that was my destination.

Horses and carts lined the front of the castle, carrying building material and tools. I slid into the tree line and watched the men go about their business, listened to unrecognizable, shouted orders as workers hustled to different sections of the structure. I needed to blend in with these Ordinaries. I took note of what they wore, then imagined myself in something similar and magically exchanged my embellished green gown for a simple gray smock and cloak, as well as little brown slippers. I added a blast of dirt to the clothing for good measure, since most of the people I saw were filthy. My wings disappeared, along with my pointed ears and slanted green eyes, and I made myself visible.

"You there!" called a man from above. "What are you doing out here?"

Startled, I turned and dropped my cowl. With his strange accent, I barely understood his words.

"Guards! Open the gate and let the lady inside."

A heavy wooden door ground open, and two elderly women hustled toward me. They chattered in a language I didn't understand, but they wore smiles on their faces. I let them usher me into the castle, then along a hall and into one of the many rooms. They helped me out of my dirt-covered clothes, and the older lady took them away. She made a downward motion with her hands, but I had no idea what she was trying to tell me until the burly woman arrived, carrying a round basin. She filled it with buckets of water then motioned for me to get in. Someone gave me a little tan-colored bar then dunked my hand in the warm liquid, showing me what they meant. Small bubbles emerged when I rubbed the little bar, and a flowery fragrance filled the air. I smiled, understanding that they wanted me to bathe, and lowered myself into the water.

When I looked into their eyes, I suddenly realized I could both hear and understand their thoughts. Could I hear all Ordinaries' thoughts? Opening my mind to this revelation, I clearly heard the name of the white-haired woman: *Elizabeth.* She wondered why I'd been outside the castle and where I had come from. The other woman, *Ann,* who had gone to clean my clothes, thought I would make a beautiful bride for one of her sons. I smothered a chuckle at the thought that I would have left Fairyland so I could marry here in … where was I?

England: an island country. In AD 43 the Roman conquest of Britain began. The Anglo-Saxons, a collection of various Germanic peoples, established several kingdoms which became the primary powers in what is called England.

I blinked, entirely confused. Where had that information come from?

Someone knocked on the door, startling me from my thoughts. A little girl entered and handed Ann a neat stack of green material, then she smiled at me. She reminded me of Brea, with her sweet face and that glint of mischief twinkling in her eyes. The thought made me sad. When I'd left Fairyland, I hadn't even thought about what would happen to Brea, or what she'd think about all this. *Some friend I am.*

"Doesn't she talk?" the girl asked.

Incredibly, now I could both read their thoughts *and* understand what they were saying. Very convenient! Maybe I'd eventually be able to speak their language as well, but I wasn't ready to try.

"No, Mary. Not a word yet." Elizabeth shrugged. "Maybe she will when she's ready."

"She's probably traumatized from being outside for so long," Ann suggested. "I know I would be. So let's leave her alone, and maybe we can get to know her later." She shooed Mary out the door, then turned back to me. "We'll leave you for now," she said slowly, her voice slightly louder than it had been, "and I'll be back with some food. I bet you're famished."

Both women left me in the now cold barrel of water, and I started to wonder *when* I was. I already knew the *where*. Maybe when everyone slept I could take a look around this place, explore, and get some answers.

I rose from the bath and used my glamour to instantly dry off, then I dressed in the long green tunic Mary had brought, cinched at the waist with a gold ribbon. I walked around the large room and leaned out an open window, wanting to view the expansive countryside of rolling pastures and hills. Small dots sprinkled the landscape, and I presumed they were horses and cattle—maybe even wild animals.

As soon as my hands touched the stone sill, my mind filled with information.

Windsor Castle: a royal residence built at Windsor in the county of Berkshire, designed to protect Norman dominance around London, and to oversee a strategically important part of the River Thames.

I passed by a small cabinet and stopped at a mirror, where I stood for a while, shocked to see the unfamiliar reflected face. My vibrant green eyes—unaccustomedly round—glittered like emeralds under my black hair, which was now a neat, short cut. My back was smooth, with no sign of wings sprouting from between my shoulder blades. I was still tall but slender, with just the right amount of muscle tone to have leg and arm definition. I had to admit: I looked fantastic. I turned back to the door, and when I didn't hear anyone coming I pictured myself the way I would look in Fairyland. In my mind the two images melted together and showed the striking young woman.

The door opened, and Mary poked her head in. "Good. You're out of the bath." She stepped into the room, carrying a tray. "Here. I brought you some food. I begged my mother to let me bring it in, because we do not get many new female visitors here."

I smiled at her, encouraging her to keep talking. My smile lit hers even brighter.

"I'm Mary," she said.

She laid the platter on a corner table, and I walked over to peer at the drab-colored 'food'. Mary must have noticed my expression, for she came over to stand beside me.

"You look confused," she said. "Don't you know what this is?"

I shook my head, and her eyes widened with amazement. "This is chicken," she said. "You really have never had it before?"

I shook my head again.

"What? How can you not have had this? It is a staple around here." She pointed at the platter again. "And this is a green apple. It's okay, but I prefer the red ones."

I reached for the familiar apple then wondered if the food here would be safe for me to eat. I wouldn't get sick, would I? Taking a small bite, I chewed, swallowed, then smiled. It tasted exactly the same as our green apples did back home.

"Here." Mary handed me a cup. "Drink this. It is wine."

I do know wine. I smiled my thanks and drank enough to quench my thirst.

She stuck out her bottom lip, watching me. "I can't have it yet because I'm too young," she said, then she tilted her head and peered closely at me. "You don't say much, do you?" She shrugged. "That is all right. I talk enough for everyone."

I heard her say in her mind: *That's what they tell me, anyway.*

"I am always being told to be quiet," Mary said out loud. She walked to the bed and sat, still grinning at me. "You are really pretty, you know." Her inner monologue continued: *I wish I looked like you.* "I bet you are married." *If I had your hair, I would be.* "I hate my brown hair. Maybe I will cut mine short like yours. You do not mind, do you?"

I shook my head, smiling. She did talk a lot, but I liked her. I took a breath then dared myself to speak. "Would you like to show me around?" I asked. I grinned coyly at her look of surprise. "And my name is Sidelle."

Chapter 14

"You do talk! I knew it!" she exclaimed, looking victorious. "Everyone else said you were mute, but not me. I told them you just did not want to talk to them." She giggled. "I am glad you spoke your first words to me, because now I have something that my stinky brother does not." *He gets everything because he's the oldest, and that's not fair at all. What a beautiful and unusual name she has!* "You are not from around here, are you?"

The inner ramblings of the child amused me, but I needed to focus, to get on with gathering information. "No, I am not." I extended my arm for her, and we walked out of the room. We made our way downstairs, passing colorful tapestries and painted murals of landscapes which stretched from floor to ceiling. I tugged on Mary's arm so that we came to a stop in front of a random mural.

"What's this about?" I asked.

She told me who some of the people in the mural were and a little about the nature scenes. As I listened, the new information came alive in my head, and my mind tingled. Information she hadn't even told me sprouted and grew, and I suddenly knew everything about each man, woman, and family in the paintings. I even knew the actual location depicted by the painting.

I was sure that new trick of mine would eventually come in pretty handy.

The tour included a brief visit to the kitchen, the throne room, and the massive library. We lingered there the longest, as I kept selecting bound books, scrolls, and maps to inspect. Whenever my fingers touched a book spine or a drawing, its facts and history appeared in my head. I had no idea how many records I viewed, but I could have looked at everything.

Mary seemed impatient, constantly pacing around the room.

"Would you like to move on?" I asked.

She heaved a sigh. "Yes! I thought you would never ask." She led me outside, and we stopped in the middle of a courtyard. "This is my favorite place in the whole castle," she said, and I admired its beauty. A towering oak stood in the center of the courtyard, surrounded by multi-colored flowers. In each of the four directions, groomed paths led to the lone tree. It reminded me of home.

"This is beautiful. Thank you for sharing it with me."

"It will be dark soon, so we should get you back inside," she said, "but I wanted to show you this. I'm out here a lot, and now you can come visit me whenever you want to." She looked curiously at me. "What job are you going to do while you stay here?"

I hadn't even thought of that. "I am not sure. Does everyone have a job?"

"Yes, unless you are the King."

Ah, the man who built the castle. *William was Duke of Normandy. As William I, the first Norman King of England, he defeated and killed the last Anglo-Saxon*

King at the Battle of Hastings. Upon his father's death, William was recognized as heir and crowned king.

"Come on," Mary said. "I will help you get back to your room."

A guard stood watch outside my door. He wore a silver helmet and chest armor over black leggings and a faded red tunic. Off to the side, a long spear leaned against the wall.

"Where have you been, Princess?" he demanded. "How am I supposed to guard you—"

"I—" we both said.

Mary and I glanced at each other in surprise, then I nodded and let her speak. *I'm not a Princess in this world. I have to remember that.*

"I took Sidelle around the castle," Mary replied. "She wanted to see the library."

"That's fine, but your father—"

"Please do not tell him!"

Frowning, the guard grabbed her arm and tried to wrestle her from my grasp. "I do not think you should go off by yourself with a stranger."

She clung to me, twisting out of the guard's hands. "She is not a stranger. She is my friend."

I marveled at that. I'd been here for half a day, and already someone had called me their friend.

Heavy footsteps echoed in the hallway, and I turned to see two more guards approaching. They addressed me directly. "You are requested by the King," said one. "Follow us."

The first guard took Mary's arm again. "And you will stay with me. I will escort you to your room."

I nodded reassuringly at Mary, and she finally released my hand.

The guards escorted me through the castle to the throne room. A pair of heavy double doors opened, and there sat King William, relaxing in a throne made of solid gold. His clothes were similar to what we all wore, but upon closer inspection I could see the quality of the knit was finer and his tunic was a deeper shade of blue. He wore a small gold crown.

"Approach," he commanded, "stranger from afar."

I dropped into a low curtsy before him.

He observed me for a moment before he spoke again. In my head, I heard, *She is tall for a woman, and very pretty.*

"They tell me you do not speak."

"No, Your Highness," I said, not looking him in the eye in case these people saw that as a disrespectful approach. I decided to play it safe by behaving meekly. "I speak. I was simply confused for a while. I thought it best if I gathered my wits first."

"From whence did you come, and what business had you outside the gates?"

Keep it vague, I warned myself. "I have traveled far and could go no farther when I stumbled across your magnificent castle. I am grateful for your kindness and for allowing me to stay the night."

He rose and his massive cloak settled around him. "What is your age?"

"I am ten and five years," I bluffed, hoping that wasn't too old or too young. I was only just beginning to understand the Ordinaries' concept of time.

He stepped down from the dais and came toward me. I kept my chin down. "And why is it you travel alone?"

"My parents are no longer alive, and I have no siblings."

He circled slowly around me, and I fought the urge to run. I didn't like the close observation. He toyed with a short strand of my hair, testing my boundaries. "How long do you plan to stay?"

I shivered when his hand swept my cheek. "No longer than you command."

Good answer, I heard in my head. *She must have lived around royalty, though I have no idea where that might have been.*

"My Mary has taken a liking to you," he said quietly. "I do not allow the staff to play with my daughter since they are here to do a job, not to entertain her; however, since you have no official duties, I would like you to accompany Mary. Be her friend, tutor, and confidante. Whatever she may need."

"As you wish," I replied, bowing again and wondering if this new adventure might help me in my search for The Redeemer.

Chapter 15

Early spring of 1666

I stayed with Mary and watched her grow. I became her advisor and was both proud and happy when she married. Since the king had obviously accepted me, no one pressed me about my background, and after a while they stopped even thinking of me as a stranger in their land.

Using my glamour, I aged myself along with Mary so I would not raise suspicions. But she continued to age. She was only human, after all.

After her passing, I was desperately unhappy and couldn't remain at the castle. I roamed between forts and sanctuaries throughout England and on the mainland, which was called Europe. I stayed in chateaus in France, palaces in Austria, and castles in Norway, but I made sure I relocated every twenty-five years or so. I took on different appearances when I moved, including clothing style, height, and weight, but I always kept two things constant: my green eyes and black hair. I wanted something to remind me of who I really was.

During my years with the Ordinaries, I learned a vast amount of information, saw many things built and destroyed, and knew various kings and queens. Every now and then I ran into another Summer fairy, also on the hunt for The Redeemer. It was nice to see a familiar face and talk about home, but we eventually parted ways and moved on with our search. The world seemed much smaller then.

I occasionally returned to Fairyland, checking in with my father to provide updates and let him know I had not yet located The Redeemer. I was relieved that Brea completely understood I was following orders. She didn't make me feel badly about leaving her behind.

For a while I considered England to be my second home—maybe because I'd met my first Ordinary friend there—and I frequently found myself returning to that island. Over time, London became a city known for renovation and inspiration, and people flocked there for jobs. Society women dressed in long, flowing gowns, and color became a way to express one's self. My fashion tastes changed as well. After centuries of wearing leggings, I was happy to wear beautiful ball gowns again, like the ones I used to despise.

In fact, as I lived through centuries and cultures, I realized I loved the world of fashion. When I arrived in London one day, I decided to search for a new area where I could stay and be part of the fashion world. As I passed a crowded shop, I opened the glass door and breathed in a strange fragrance. It reminded me of how the lower floors of my father's castle smelled right after a rain.

A young lady with fire red hair sat on a stool behind the counter. She glanced up from her sewing, smiling. "Hello," she said.

"Good afternoon." I walked through the main aisle toward her, my fingers skimming over a pale blue dress. Just by touch I instantly learned everything about the craft of sewing. "Are you the owner of this lovely establishment?"

"I am."

Over the centuries, I had developed another amazing skill. If I focused, I could persuade most Ordinaries to change their mind by suggesting they do what I wanted. I called it Mind Walking. I didn't use my ability very often, but when I did it was very useful. From the look and feel of this shop, I really wanted to work here, and I was determined to make the woman like me.

"Wonderful." I touched a gold feather curving elegantly over a wide brimmed hat. "I am looking for employment and am wondering if you are in need of assistance."

You are seeking an apprentice, I suggested.

The woman stared directly into my eyes for a second, and I watched, mesmerized, as her pupils shrank to tiny black holes, then dilated to almost cover the whites.

"I am," she said, but she wasn't easily swayed. "What is your name? Do you have any prior experience?"

"Uh, yes." I blinked, surprised to be questioned. Usually my mind power convinced them easily. "My name is Sidelle Amistad, and my experience is quite extensive, actually."

"Where are my manners?" She laid her sewing on her lap and brushed her palms against the sides of her yellow dress. "I'm Jessa Venator."

"Pleasure to meet you," I said, returning her smile. "When can I start?" I tried to project into her mind: *In a few days so I can line up some projects for you to work on.*

"Tomorrow," she said decisively. "Yes, that will work." She cocked her head to one side. "Are you looking for a place to stay, too?"

Yes, I am! I urged into her mind.

Her cheeks turned a rosy pink. "I'm sorry. I assumed you were not married, since I don't see a ring on your finger. Then I realized that someone as beautiful as you would be married, of course. So you must already have a place to stay."

Something wasn't right here. She should be repeating what I was suggesting to her. "No, actually, I *am* looking for a place to stay. Do you know of someplace?"

She smiled broadly, lighting her dark eyes. "As a matter of fact, I need someone to share my flat. I know this sounds strange, and I just met you, but you seem nice and—"

"I'd love to see where you live," I said.

"And your things?"

"A friend is holding my belongings until I can find a place of my own." In reality, I didn't lug anything around with me. I conjured anything I needed: food, clothes, even shelter if I couldn't find it.

"Perfect. Well, I'm done here, so let me close up for the night, and we can be on our way." Jessa tidied the small shop, drew the shades, and locked the front door while I waited. "Where does your friend live? Or we can go to my flat first and send a courier to get your things."

"Lead the way."

I sidestepped to let her pass in front of me, but her arm touched mine as she brushed by. A jolt coursed through me, and I was suddenly on guard against danger. If I'd been in my regular form, my wings would be spread out.

Despite my reservations, I walked with her along on cobblestoned streets, meandered by a park fountain, then slowly made an uphill climb into a posh neighborhood, past row after row of slender wooden houses. We talked a little bit about ourselves, but not much. I tried, but I couldn't pick up anything from her mind.

She stopped in front of a large stone house that was unlike the rest. The three story mansion had obviously been built much earlier than the others, but it was well maintained.

"You live here?" I exclaimed, taking in the beautiful old building. "I thought you said you lived in a flat."

She shrugged. "I do, but it's more like a community of sorts. A lot of other people live in the same building, but we have our own doors. You'll get used to it after a while."

"Do you all know each other?"

Jessa nodded. "Unfortunately, yes. They're my family members. I'm the oldest from a pack of rambunctious boys who behave more like dogs than men."

"If you live with your family, then why are you looking for a flat mate? That seems—"

Jessa held up her hand. "I know what you are going to say."

She did?

"This was the only way my father would let me live alone," she explained.

I definitely understood that.

"He constructed the inner doors to allow me some privacy." She stopped in front of a solid wooden door, pulled out a brass key, and stepped inside.

My eyes adjusted to the dimly lit grand room, and I saw a full kitchen off to one side. A seating area that overlooked the city through massive windows took up the other side of the room. Everything was done in pristine white marble. My guess was that it had been imported from Italy. Candles hung from the ceiling and lined the walls in gold fixtures.

"The bedrooms and the bathroom are down the hall," Jessa said. "I have the room on the right."

I was in awe. The advancement of their way of life astounded me. I knew of some places in Asia where they had indoor toilets, but to see it here in London really impressed me.

"Wasn't what you were expecting, is it?" Jessa asked, interrupting my thoughts. "I know it's a lot to take in. Here, let me show you your room, and you can decide if all this is worth it or not."

She led me to the bedroom on the left and opened the door to a beautiful room made of more white marble. The view out the large window overlooked the river, and I was mystified as to why she hadn't chosen this room for herself.

"I'll take it." I smiled, and it was the first genuine smile I'd given in a long time. "All my belongings will fit nicely in here."

"Good," she replied. "Now I must get ready for dinner, or else my father is going to smash something. We gather to eat at night. You should come with me."

"No," I said shyly. "It's a family thing."

"It is . . . and it isn't. I have a feeling you and I will be hanging around each other a lot, so you might as well meet them."

I shook my head again. "Another time. I would like to get my belongings and find a place for everything so I can make this room feel like home."

"I understand. We can have dinner together tomorrow."

Chapter 16

The next morning at sunrise, I awoke to the sound of glasses and cutlery scraping against plates. I dragged myself out of the pile of pillows I'd created for my bed then went to investigate. I peeked around the corner and spotted the silhouette of a man standing in front of the kitchen window, his back to me.

The sweet aroma of baked goods wafted to my nose. My glamour wrapped a robe around me to hide my white night dress, and I stepped into the hallway.

"Morning," the man said quietly, not turning. "I hope I didn't wake you. Jessa is a heavy sleeper." He glanced over and waved me toward him. "You must be Sidelle."

I hesitated then reasoned that he was probably safe. A thief wouldn't have brought breakfast. "I am. And you are?"

"Jessa's father, Gage Venator. I bring her breakfast every morning." He smiled sheepishly. "I can't seem to let her grow up. I still think of her as my little girl. I'm glad she has you around now."

I stood at the wall opposite and studied him out of the corner of my eye. He was extremely tall with broad shoulders, and he radiated a definite "don't mess with me" aura.

"What does that mean?" I asked, reaching for a buttered roll. "She just met me yesterday."

He chuckled low in his throat and shook his head slowly, as if he were savoring a joke. "I'd heard the rumors, but I had to come see for myself."

He inhaled and I watched his massive chest move beneath his shirt. *Jeez! I just checked out Jessa's father!* To be fair, he was incredibly young looking, like he really couldn't be her dad. Maybe an older brother, but certainly not a father.

He glanced at me, and I blushed. "Um, see what?"

"You, of course." He stared directly at me. "And here you are, right here in my kitchen. Well, it's actually Jessa's kitchen, but still my house."

I had the distinct impression that he knew exactly who I was. But that was impossible, wasn't it? I shook my head. "I don't know what you mean. I—"

"Your secret is safe with my family as long as you keep ours."

I crossed my arms, defensive. "And yours would be . . . what, exactly?"

He looked surprised. "You've never run into us before?"

"I really have no idea what you're talking about," I said flatly. "I'm not very worldly."

"That's not what Jessa said." Gage tilted his head slightly, and his black hair brushed his shoulder. "She said you used to live in London, down by the river. I happen to know there hasn't been a private residence there since, well, let's just say a really long time. Unless you meant the palace."

I dropped my breakfast and watched it roll onto the floor. My stomach followed. I'd been careful, hadn't I? I'd never slipped in my stories, only giving them just enough information . . .

But maybe these Ordinaries weren't ordinary at all. Why hadn't I been able to suggest things through Jessa's mind?

"I see you're confused." Jessa, still dressed in her nightgown, entered the kitchen and pulled out a chair. "Don't you think we're a little different from other people?" She grabbed a gooey pastry from the basket and grinned at me. "I saw you when you stepped in my store. You felt something was off."

"Yes." There was no point in lying.

She stuffed the whole thing into her little mouth then opened her mouth to speak, but Gage stopped her.

"Don't talk with your mouth full," he said. "It's rude."

"I wasn't going to." She giggled then swallowed some of the food, but apparently not all of it because both her cheeks still bulged.

"Who exactly do you think I am?" I asked.

Jessa chewed some more, then suddenly glanced at her father and started frantically shaking her head. Her arms flailed, and she jumped to her feet.

"Are you choking?" I cried, running to her side.

I slapped her back—hard—then I panicked, seeing her eyes turn black. I hit her again, and this time I did it with a little too much force. Her small body flew forward.

Her father caught her, and his head swiveled in my direction. He seemed to be crouching in a strange, almost protective stance.

A low growl rose from both of them, and I stepped back, confused. Both of their bodies shuddered, then Jessa fell to her hands and knees and her father followed. I watched in utter shock as black fur sprouted through Gage's clothes, and tufts of red hair peeked through the sleeves of Jessa's nightgown.

Then their clothes disappeared altogether.

I stood paralyzed, my mouth hanging open.

Chapter 17

Gage now stood on four paws. Incredibly, he had transformed into a huge wolf with blazing red eyes. Jessa's body did the same, but she was red and much shorter in height. They advanced toward me, snarling, and I retreated another step. I hadn't felt the need for my wings in centuries, but my back itched now.

I stepped toward the door. "I'm not here to hurt you," I said, trying to stay calm. "I thought Jessa was—"

The black wolf howled, cutting off my excuse. The two fanned out and began to stalk me from both directions. I reached for the doorknob, but it was locked. I was trapped.

My wings sprang from my back as I kicked off the wall, fluttering and wrapping around me, free at last. Until now I had never thought about needing defensive tactics. I waved my hand, magically halting the wolves in place, then I conjured my clothes, changing into better battle attire: pants and a tunic.

The wolves didn't stay frozen for long, then the red one howled and sat. The black one still watched me, but he didn't take another step.

See? Jessa's soft voice rang in my head. *We were right about you.*

Werewolves. So they *did* exist. I had heard rumors centuries before, but I had forgotten since I'd never run into them. They hadn't hurt me, but it turned out this was the best way for them to show me what they were. I apologized for hitting Jessa, explaining that I'd thought she was choking on her breakfast. They, in turn, expounded on why they'd snarled. Instinct had come first, then they'd overpowered the urge to cause harm.

Gage was England's Alpha, and Jessa, since she was the oldest female, was the Beta. While I lived with them, I learned a lot about pack life and their lives; though I was sure they kept some information private to outsiders. They, being Naturals—what they called themselves—could block some glamour, and though they never told me exactly which of my abilities they could avoid, I already knew they didn't take to my Mind Walking.

Jessa and I worked side by side for many days, which turned into weeks. Months passed, and we became close friends. I guessed living together helped, too. When we were alone in the store, I used my glamour and was instantly done with the days' orders, so we spent those extra hours gossiping, telling stories, and sharing our dreams. I came to think of her pack as my other family. They often went out at night, when they did, they left me alone to continue my pursuit of The Redeemer.

One day Gage called a pack meeting, which I attended. I joined them all in a room I hadn't known existed in the main house and sat at a conference table that held twenty members. Floor to ceiling maps hung on the walls, marked with red clusters of dots. Upon closer inspection, I recognized familiar street names and the layout of London and Paris. Some of the pack members moved their seats away, and others rose and stood against the table when I took my seat. I ignored them.

"Some of you may be wondering why I invited Sidelle to this meeting." Gage's strong voice silenced the room. "Sidelle is a fairy, and she means us no harm. We consider her to be family."

Somewhat reluctantly, the pack members returned to their places at the table, allowing me in.

Now that had been established, Gage made eye contact with each of his pack members, returning to the reason for the meeting. "I'm asking each of you to fulfill your duty and your oath to me. The rumblings around town have worsened, and I need more eyes and bodies to keep the Ordinaries safe."

He spoke with such authority, I could see why he was Alpha.

"Our small group can no longer hold them at bay," Gage continued. "We are on the verge of being overpowered by the DKs, and I will not allow that to happen. Not on my watch."

I raised my hand. "What are DKs?" Everyone stared at me, and I felt my cheeks grow warm.

"Sidelle." The Alpha nodded. "Thank you for reminding me. Let me back up and explain so everyone in this room is clear. Werewolves are an old species," he said, "created from the wolf and mixed with Angel Light. The grace of the angel gave the animal more intellect, but since the Ordinaries have advanced, we also had to evolve. Our primary reason for existence is to keep Demon Knights—DKs—in check."

"What are they?" I asked.

"There are many theories about them. Some say they are fallen angels, but others claim they are just another race."

"How did they get here?"

"Every Hallow's Eve the veil between earth and hell weakens, and some demons manage to escape into earth's realm. Until recently not many had come through, but more and more have found a way. We werewolves are spread thin since we are now covering both Ireland and Scotland."

I was enthralled. "How do you know the difference between a Demon Knight and an Ordinary?" I looked around the room. "Do they look different?"

Gage tapped his nose. "We can smell them. *You* might even be able to see their true form."

"What does that mean?"

"You might be able to see what they look like under their skin. They look and act like an Ordinary, but underneath they are still demons." He shrugged. "Since I'm not a fairy, I don't know what you will see or how you will know."

"Do you kill them?" I asked, unsure. "Because I'm not sure I can do that. I've never ended someone's life before, even if they are evil. We have some bad fairies—we co-exist with Winter and we *hate* Winter—but that doesn't mean I could kill them."

He nodded grimly. "Yes. You have to behead them in some way. If it helps you, they don't actually die. Their bodies disappear from earth, but they will reform in hell, ready to fight again."

"What if I can't—"

His eyes narrowed. "Isn't that why you're here? To help control the demon population?"

"No, not exactly. I'm on a secret mission for the angels."

"Whatever the reason," he said, ignoring my reply, "I am asking you to help us, since you are a member of my pack."

"Of course," I said. "I will do as you ask. I would do

anything for you and your pack."

"Good. We will leave tonight to do city sweeps, and I'll pair you with Jessa. She'll teach you the ropes. Maybe she can learn a few tricks from you, too."

After the meeting, Jessa led us back to her shop. On the way, she talked about fighting techniques, stances, and weaponry, which really surprised me. I hadn't realized she knew so much about all this, since she'd been so quiet during the meeting. Being the Beta, I'd suspected she knew a fair amount, but she blew my mind with the extent of her knowledge. When she spoke like this she was like a whole different person.

"I'm not sure what you can do with your magic," Jessa said, "but I can show you some quick defensive maneuvers."

"My magic is called glamour," I told her, "and I can do pretty much anything with it. I can manipulate the weather, move objects, and I can learn how to do something in a blink of an eye." I pointed to the park up ahead. "Let's stop there and see if I can Mind Walk you. That way I could learn all the fighting skills I will need."

"Mind walk?"

"Yes. It's where I take a peek inside your head and get all the information I need."

She frowned. "That doesn't sound nice."

"It's not." I lowered my head. "But with so little time, I need to. Up until now, I haven't been able to do that on you, but if you open your mind it might work."

We got to the park and sat on one of the stone benches, overlooking the Thames.

"What do you need me to do?" Jessa asked, obviously concerned. "Is it going to hurt?"

"You won't feel a thing," I assured her. "What I need is for you to think of everything you've learned over the years about fighting, weapon handling, and general demon knowledge."

She hesitated. "Are you going to read my mind about other things as well?"

"I promise I'll only take pertinent stuff on fighting and demons."

After Jessa reluctantly agreed, I drew in a deep breath and placed my hands on either side of her head. Normally I didn't have to do it this way, but I figured direct contact would work better. I closed my eyes and felt the moment when Jessa released her thoughts to me. After that all I had to do was let my mind wander through images of Jessa learning various tactics, stances, and maneuvers.

Then I went a little farther and found information about demons.

Knights: responsible for causing most of the so-called 'manmade' destruction in the world, like the Holy Wars. When knights are killed on earth, they don't die. Their bodies disintegrate and reappear in Hell. How long it takes for their bodies to regenerate depends on what sort of bodily damage had been inflicted on them during a battle. Knights are susceptible to human weaknesses.

Marquises: mid-level demons typically found in small groups. They are the fighters of Hell. They are ruthless and brutal, and they're also expert swordsmen. They start 'natural disasters', like floods, erupting volcanoes, and fires.

The Prince of Demons: no information known.

The King: The Seraph angels locked him in a cage in Hell during his fall from Heaven. He still rules, but can't get out.

All this information took mere seconds to load into my brain. Now it was a matter of utilizing the information and making my body perform the moves. I removed my hands from Jessa's face and stood.

"Is it done?" she asked.

"Yes."

"Huh. I didn't feel a thing."

"Told you. Actually, you wouldn't even have known what I was doing if I hadn't touched you." I rolled my shoulders back, stretching a bit. "Okay. Let's go find some demons."

We wandered up and down the streets, patrolling for anything that seemed out of place. I still didn't know what to look for or how the demons would appear to me, but I assumed Jessa would let me know. Every voice and noise put me on edge. My body hummed with excitement but was wrapped so tight I jerked at every sound.

We traveled to an uninhabited section of London, near the edge of the city, and though we were blanketed by darkness, I could see just fine. An eerie silence hung in the air, and my wings itched to come out. Something was going to happen soon. I could feel it.

Suddenly a tower of barrels tipped over near the door of a building, crashing and rolling to the ground with a huge noise. Jessa flattened against the stone wall and motioned for me to follow. She leaned in and whispered in my ear, "They're inside."

How do you know? I asked her silently. When she didn't respond I whispered back, "Open your mind so I can communicate with you."

She shot me a puzzled glance, and I flashed my eyes at her, urging her to do as I suggested. Eventually I felt her mental wall lower.

Hey, there.

"Whoa!" Her hands went to her head. "You're really in there!"

How do you know they're in there? I asked again.

"I can smell them," Jessa whispered.

Okay, so how do you want to do this?

She nodded, still smiling at the sense of having me right there in her head. "All right. We'll look around the back to see how many there are. You need to stick with me until I know you can handle yourself. "

Why don't I just pop in there and find out?

"Wait." She blinked at me, looking impressed. "Can you be unseen?"

I nodded. *I'll be right back.*

In an instant I arrived inside the shipping warehouse, but I remained invisible. I counted five demons who looked just like Ordinaries, until I inspected them closer. Their glowing red eyes were the first things to give them away. Then I looked deeper and it became obvious what they were. Under the demons' pale human skin, their mangled bodies were red and oozing with black pus. I'd never seen anything like them.

I wondered briefly if they had ever come across a fairy before.

I reappeared beside Jessa. *Five. And yeah, I can see through them. They're disgusting.*

She nodded then motioned for me to follow. We snuck around the corner, careful not to touch anything that might cause a sound, and found an open door around the second turn. Silently, she unsheathed her sword and held it in front of her.

You're not going in as a wolf?

She shook her head. "Takes too much energy. I can handle these with a sword."

I thought about that. The problem with that approach was that when she was in human form, like right now, she would be susceptible to injuries . . . even death.

"Are you ready?" she whispered, her eyes steady.

I had to believe she knew what she was doing. After

all, she'd been fighting these things for a long time
before I'd come along. If anything happened, I'd just
have to protect her. I nodded. *Yes.*

She pointed at me and motioned to the right, then
she jabbed her finger against her own chest and gestured
to the left. I nodded. She lifted her hand then lowered
her fingers one by one, counting down. When the last
one dropped, we crept inside the door. I targeted my two
marks right away, deciding how best to attack. My heart
raced. I could do this. I had to. They were demons, I
reminded myself, not Ordinaries.

In the next moment, Jessa sprinted straight into her
group of three demons. She caught one by surprise and
slashed his chest in half while I watched, stunned. I
hoped that was close enough to cutting off its head. The
other two demons scrambled into a defensive stance, and
Jessa's arms and legs whirled, connecting with their
stomachs, heads and backs. She was amazing to watch.

The demons I had targeted reacted immediately after
their brethren fell, going on the offensive. They looked
at each other, then at me. The one on my right made a
fist and slapped it against his other hand. The left demon
drew a handmade knife from his belt and seemed about
to approach when they noticed I didn't have a weapon.
Their smiles were priceless. They assumed I was going
to be easy. After that, they figured they could just
dispose of Jessa.

They wouldn't get a chance to even touch Jessa. Not
on my watch. I stood in place, letting them approach. I
even waved them forward, and the stupid creatures took
the bait, advancing confidently from both sides.

Nope, they had apparently never come across a fairy.
I grinned. This could actually be fun. One of them
chuckled, anticipating an easy fight, and that was my
cue. My left hand twisted, and both demons flew

backwards against the wall, their bodies crumpling to the floor. A few seconds later, one got to his feet and shook his head, then focused on me. He charged, but he didn't stand a chance.

I liked fighting this way. If I kept it up, no one would actually die by my physical hand, and I could live with that. Gathering my glamour, I created a wind vortex then slammed it against him with all my might. His body crashed alongside a support beam, and I heard an undeniable crack from his back, which told me he would no longer walk.

The other demon, seeing his friend howling and twitching on the ground, ran at me, a knife slashing in the air before him. I redirected the wind and blew his weapon from his hands, rendering it useless, then conjured a couple of handfuls of pebbles which I tossed at his feet. He slid, lost his balance, and fell backward, cracking his skull on a stone I'd strategically placed there. Like his friend, he would not get up again.

I looked back at Jessa, who had disposed of her three demons. Curious to see how she'd dispatched them, I searched for her prey, but they no longer lay on the floor. Jessa leaned against the wall, watching my performance. When she saw me looking for her, she kicked off and strode toward me.

"That was awesome!" she exclaimed. "If I'd known you could do all that, I wouldn't have had you do the Mind Walk." She bent over the demon with the broken back and sliced smoothly through his jugular. "He doesn't need to be in pain," she explained. "Father says to end the DKs quickly." Grinning, she walked past me and said over her shoulder, "I think you're going to be our new favorite weapon."

Chapter 18

My confidence grew after the easy defeat of the DKs. No longer was I some helpless princess. Both the actual fighting experience and Jessa's shared knowledge helped me focus my attention and hone my fighting skills. I was confident I could take on every demon that crossed my path, and I became a bad-ass, fight-finding fairy. For the first time ever, I felt as if my life really had purpose.

Jess and I secured the streets every night. Sometimes we went alone, and other times I was part of a small group. Some of the other pack members said they wanted to partner with me so they could see firsthand all the tricks I could do. In all the time we worked together, I never saw any of them turn into their wolf form. Jessa assured me that some would when they patrolled in the woods or outside of the city.

Demons spread the word throughout London, saying the werewolves were working with a ruthless witch. I created a reputation for myself, but with the good came the bad. Now that I was known, more DKs were gunning for me. We noticed an increase in their numbers over the months, and my guess was they wanted revenge.

One morning in September, Gage called a pack meeting. We assembled over breakfast for the news.

"The angels say a rip in the veil occurred last night," he said grimly. "They don't know how many came through before they could seal it, but we should expect to see an increase in the demon population. So today we'll do double duty. We'll do shifts all day and well into the night until we can get some figures." He sighed. "One other thing: we don't know if any of the Marqs made it or not."

I had never gone up against a Marquises demon, so I didn't know what they looked like or what they could do to me. Sure, my mind had taken in information about them, but until I was put in a situation there was no way to know which of my glamour worked on them—if any.

We gathered around the map as Gage divided us into three factions—morning, afternoon, and evening. I was selected to be in the first and third groups, which was fine with me. I rather liked fighting the demons and was good at it. Plus, this was my small contribution to the pack while I remained on my own mission. Jessa and I teamed up for the morning patrol, and we would again later that night. Gage seemed to think nighttime would bring an increase in numbers.

No action, fights, nor skirmishes happened on my first shift, so I didn't have anything to report to the pack afterward. Maybe Gage's suspicion was correct: the demons were gathering, strategizing, and waiting for nightfall.

By darkness, things were too quiet. No one had yet seen any DKs within the city limits, so a small group of hunters was sent to the outskirts of London to check the abandoned factories, docks, and woods.

They were out there, I knew. What I didn't know was where. They had to be holed up someplace.

At ten in the evening, Jessa met me in front of her shop. I stayed shrouded in the shadows because of my reputation. Since demons didn't care if anyone found out about us, word had even spread to the Ordinaries, so they now believed a witch was in town. That meant they were on the lookout as well. I didn't need a witch hunt added to my complicated life.

"This is so strange," Jessa said, talking about the lack of demon sightings. "The angels are never wrong— or they haven't been thus far."

"I know. Something isn't right. I can feel it."

"Come on," she said, sounding resigned. "Let's go make our usual loop then call it a night."

We walked past the park, down to the river, then back up Pudding Lane. As we passed, we smelled the fresh baked goods wafting from the famous baker's shop. He made the best breads anywhere. I inhaled, imagining the buttery dough balls. I'd come to like the smell of fruits and breads best. Maybe because they reminded me of home.

"Tomorrow we should stop here for the morning rolls," I suggested.

I caught movement in the shadows and jerked back, silently grabbing Jessa's hand. She nodded. I approached carefully, taking my time and opening myself to the surroundings, calling my glamour around me. I held my breath when a black cat jumped from a stack of barrels, knocking them over and spilling their contents to the ground. I righted one, then my back twitched, and the hairs on my arms rose.

Stillness had fallen over the air like a blanket. My body had frozen in place, but my eyes darted in all directions.

An indistinguishable form floated out from behind the gnarled trunk of a tree. The hood of its dark cloak was raised, so I couldn't make out the facial features. A sword was strapped to its back.

"I found you," a low voice hissed. *"Fairy."*

He drew closer, and I saw how truly gruesome the cloaked newcomer was. Long black hair hung from under his hood, and hollowed spaces took the place of eyes.

"Yeah, you did." I puffed my chest. "So what?"

"Sidelle," Jessa whispered behind me. "That's a Marquises Demon." She tugged on my arm. "I have to let the pack know and get reinforcements. I can't take one on by myself. I'll be back as soon as I can with help!" Before I could say anything, she backed up and ran toward her home.

"Figures your little friend would turn tail," the demon said casually. "Truth is, we don't show our faces much. There hasn't really been a need . . . until now. And so here we are."

"We? There are more of you?" I asked. "How many escaped your hellish prison?"

His cackle was low and guttural. "I can't spoil the surprise now, can I?" He drew his sword from its sheath. "Are you ready to die, fairy?"

He didn't wait for an answer but slid toward me, swinging at my head. I ducked and materialized a sword of my own, ready to block his next strike. The force of the impact twisted my arm and threw me off balance, but I shook the tension from my fingers then gripped the hilt again. With my free hand, I conjured my glamour and created fog, blanketing the streets with a heavy haze. I couldn't see anything in front of me, so I relied on my senses.

The lack of vision didn't hamper the demon. He kept swinging as if he knew exactly where I stood. I obviously needed to change tactics. I parried with him more, all the while gathering my magic until the sky flashed with lightning and rain pounded the ground around us.

His mocking voice cut through the night. "You think a little water and mist is going to stop me?"

"Why don't you try taking on someone your own size?"

A new voice rung over the crack of thunder, and I stared at an intense yellow light as it circled the ground, cutting through the fog. Before me stood an angel, his golden wings wrapped around his body, his silver sword extended.

He turned to me. "I heard you needed some help."

"You heard wrong," I said lightly, annoyed by his arrogance. "I was just about to dispose of this rodent."

The angel's light faded the demon to a shade of gray and froze him in place. The Marquises coughed, helpless.

"There are more where he came from." The angel glanced around. "We should team up. My Light won't hold him forever."

I lowered my sword. "I already have a partner."

"Jessa? Yeah, she sent me to you."

Something about his tone made me angry. I gave a mock curtsy. "Fine. If it'll get you off my case, then by all means, have at it."

Within a few seconds, the Marquises demon was unfrozen and back to full strength. His face scrunched, and he huffed. I bet if he could have spewed fire in that moment, he would have. His hands formed a triangle, and he puffed a breath into it like he was cold. As if on cue, four more Marqs rose like the dead from the ground.

I gathered all my glamour and shot it directly at the demon, but it had no effect. It sailed through him and hit a tree, spraying green light all over the trunk. It fizzled like water droplets . . . which gave me an idea. If the standard elements wouldn't work, maybe something else would. I uprooted the tree and used the branches to grab the demon around the waist. It wouldn't hold him for long, but it was long enough for me to behead him. While the tree held him steady, my sword sliced through the neck. The creature's head rolled off . . . and a few seconds later it grew back.

Oh, fairy!

The angel was having just as difficult a time dealing with all the newcomers. At this rate, we would be overrun. We would have to flee if reinforcements didn't arrive soon. I didn't have much time to watch the angel fight, but I caught a few glimpses. His graceful movements reminded me of a well-choreographed dance.

A lone howl filled the night's air, and pounding footsteps sounded from far away, growing louder with each step. Help was on its way. Multiple howls answered the first, and I knew my adopted pack was closing in.

But so were even more Marquises demons. They had appeared from all directions. I wondered if I had some kind of huge target on my wings.

The screams of men and women swelled, and I was even more determined to win this fight. We had to keep the Ordinaries safe; they couldn't fight this battle. I ran toward the cries, turned the corner, and came face to face with a pack of DKs. At least my glamour worked on these demons. I blasted them with pelting water, violent wind, and intense rays of green light. I blew through their ranks like a machine, cutting, slicing, and beheading. I never looked back.

The Ordinaries' screams pushed me on, and my

angel partner soon appeared by my side. He spun into the sky, wrapped his wings around himself, and twirled—then he shot like a cannon into the stars. I caught a glimpse of a yellow light dotting the atmosphere. The clouds parted, and a mass of multi-colored, winged angels descended. They flew around the streets, gathering the Ordinaries and moving them to safety.

The gold angel dropped back to the ground. "I brought reinforcements," he said unnecessarily.

"So I see," I acknowledged.

"The Archangels will take on the Marquises. You and I are to take over corralling the Ordinaries and bring them to a safe place, or to anywhere outside the direct battlefronts. If we run into the Marqs, do the best you can, but keep moving. The pack will go where it's needed."

I raised one sardonic brow. "Who made you the boss?" I asked, but the plan did seem to be a good one. After all, someone needed to take charge, and he seemed to know what he was doing. "Have you seen Jessa? I need to make sure she's okay."

"Don't worry about her. She can take care of herself. She's with her pack." That didn't ease my gut feeling. "Look," he said, gesturing toward the street. "There's a family trapped between the houses."

We herded the Ordinaries back into one of the homes, and I swept for hiding demons but didn't find any. Finally, we could rest and mentally regroup.

"Who are you, anyway?" I asked. "And are you always so bossy?"

"I'm Kieran." He nodded. "And yes. So everyone tells me. And you must be Sidelle."

"I am. You know of me?"

"Michael told me about you."

"The Archangel?"

"The one and the only."

I walked toward the door, and Kieran followed. "How do you know him?"

"He's my mentor," he said.

"What about them?" I pointed back to the house and the Ordinaries. "Are we going to let them remember what they saw?"

He nodded. "For now." His chin jerked toward the street. "Don't worry about them. Let's get back out there. I'm sure there are more to save."

In the short time we'd been inside, Ordinaries had swarmed the streets. Some yelled, and others prayed. DKs fought on every corner, using humans as shields or prisoners while the Marquises battled in groups against the angels. Swords clanked, knives clashed, and bodies fell. Red and black blood poured onto the streets, stinking like char and poured iron.

As soon as we were outside, my wings sprang from my back, and I flew to the last location where I'd seen the pack fighting. I scanned the area but didn't see my friend. I transported myself to a few adjacent streets, following the howls, but I still couldn't see Jessa. I needed to find her.

Church bells tolled, signaling midnight. When I returned to the pack's house, I could see it had been attacked as well. Fire licked through the ceiling, burning a hole in the roof.

"Jessa!" I yelled. "Come on! We have to leave!" I ran through our apartment, tossing furniture aside, looking for her. "The building's on fire!"

The roof collapsed above me with a crash, and the flames jumped to the complex next door, setting it ablaze. Smoke crawled through each floor, suffocating the inhabitants.

I leaned out the window at the sound of coughing. "Get outside!" I shouted to my neighbor.

"I won't leave without my family!" a boy bawled through his coughs. "Dad? Mom?"

"Son! Where are you?" came his mother's anguished cry. "Get outside! Don't worry about us. We'll meet you on the street."

But I could tell the family wasn't going to make it, not with their roof already caving in. I whisked over to the young boy and flew him to the street before going back for his family. I hoped somehow he would forget I'd done this, because I had no idea how to erase his memory.

Once the family was safe, I stood back, observing the chaos. The huge bonfire still raged, and I inhaled a faint smell of gasoline settling over the city. Flashes rose on the horizon as a firestorm waited to strike, and horns blasted into the smoky night, adding to the chaos.

"There's not enough water!" someone screamed.

"Have you seen Jessa?" I shouted to a neighbor man running by. "I can't find her!"

He didn't reply. Probably never heard me over all the noise. I watched helplessly as the fire spread to the next residence and the next. The stench of pine filled the air as the timber yard burned outside the city limits. The roaring of flames almost drowned the terrified screams around me, but not quite.

"We're all going to die!" a young woman shouted.

"God, save us!"

An old woman hung out her upper floor window, her head bowed over her hands. "Our Father," she cried, "Who art in Heaven, hallowed be thy name . . . ."

The flames moved deeper into the heart of city, blooming around the Tower of London and across the London Bridge. Factories, homes, and buildings combusted, setting in motion a chain reaction with no end in sight. The sky became nearly as bright as midday, and ash rained from the sky. The wind howled, encouraging the blaze to dance into the morning hours. Eventually most of the city had burst into flames, and I feared the billowing inferno had killed everyone in its path. I could taste death in the air.

There was nothing left to do but flee England—without Jessa.

Chapter 19

For a century, Jessa's disappearance weighed on my mind. Not knowing what had happened to her still bothered me.

The Great London Fire, as it became known, destroyed three hundred and seventy-three acres of the city, starting from the Tower of London in the east and stretching across the metropolis to Fleet Street and Fetter Lane in the west. It burned thirteen thousand, two hundred houses, eighty-four churches, and forty-four company halls. Officially—and miraculously—only four people died.

But I knew what wasn't written in the papers. There was no mention of the pack, the demons, or angels. To the Eternals and the Naturals, the Great London Fire became known as The Great Battle. Many lessons were learned and written down so we wouldn't forget, though we've only had minor skirmishes since that Battle. We weren't about to be lulled into complacency, though. We knew history had a way of repeating itself.

I would always remember.

My mission remained the same: to find the Redeemer. I went to Asia to learn various martial art techniques and be educated on healing potions, then I searched two other continents, looking for opportunities. I had heard of a new land in the west, and figured I should try my luck there.

That was how and why I came to New York City. When I arrived there, I resumed the only true craft I had learned in the Ordinaries' world, becoming a well-known seamstress. After a few years, I retired from that profession and changed direction by taking the fashion industry by storm. I reinvented myself every quarter of a century, developing my business savvy and running very successful clothing, accessory, and hat stores. I loved everything about New York: the fast pace, meeting people from other countries, and the technology advancements. It all fascinated me.

By the nineteen-forties, New York was the city of all cities, and fashion became a reputable career. I studied under Vera Maxwell, Bonnie Kashin, and Anne Klein, then flew to France to learn from Coco Chanel. She never mentioned it to anyone, but it was actually my idea for her to *accidentally* spill a bottle of her perfume on a department store's floor after the store manager refused to stock it. After that, customers flocked to find out who sold that particular scent.

Kieran, my golden angel, visited me once after we met that first time. Maybe he came just to check in, or maybe he came to see if I was mentally stable enough to continue with my duties.

He told me that after The Great Battle, the angels had to wipe half of the city's occupants' minds so they didn't remember seeing angels, demons, and werewolves. After that, they had created the Void—a parallel place that lay between earth and heaven. The Void was a space where they could hide some of what went on in our world from the Ordinaries. Demons might not care who they hurt, but our mission was to protect the Ordinaries. If we took our fights to the Void, it would raise fewer concerns and suspicions.

Chapter 20

June 24, 1997, 3:26 P.M., St. Joseph, Minnesota

The tiny wail of a newborn baby vibrated deep into the earth's core. My skin hummed with it, and I wondered if The Redeemer had been born. I remembered my father had said that the earth would tell us somehow. This could be her way and I only had to listen.

A message passed through my mind in that moment. It was from Kieran: *Hell's gates are open*, he told me, *and they have unleashed the Demons. Be ready.*

Ready?

I was born ready. Bring it.

Acknowledgements

Thank you to my husband, family and friends who continue to support me in my writing endeavor; thank you!

To Jami. Thank you for being the inspiration behind Sidelle. You always make people smile by your Jami-isms and contagious laughter.

To my wonderful friend Angie, who provides me my sane moments when I need to bounce off ideas.

To the Dakota County and The Loft Literary YA Writing Group who inspire me to keep writing.

To my critique partners: Ann, Maria and Kristi. You give me words of wisdom. And yes, Maria, because of you, Sidelle's story made it to paper.

To my wonderful editors: Guinevere Graham and Jen Leigh. You help me create deeper characters we grew to love, set in a realistic, but still a make believe place.

A heartfelt thank you to Marya for another fantastic cover.

Thank You,
~Kristin~

About the Author

Kristin D. Van Risseghem grew up in a small river town in Minnesota with her parents and older sister. And after receiving a double Bachelor of Science degree from Winona State University in Paralegal and Corrections, she worked as a Paralegal for various law firms around the Twin Cities for 14 years. Then she left the legal field and is now a Senior Buyer for a technology company.

Currently, Kristin lives in Eagan with her husband and two Calico cats. She also loves attending book clubs, going shopping, and hanging out with friends. She has come to realize that she absolutely has an addiction to purses and shoes. They are her weakness and probably has way too many of both.

In the summer months, Kristin can usually be found lounging on her boat, drinking an ice cold something. Being an avid reader of YA and Women's Literature stories, she still finds time to read a ton of books in-between writing. And in the winter months, her main goal is to stay warm from the Minnesota cold!

Kristin's books are published by Kasian Publishing.

Dear Reader,

I hope you enjoyed *The Masquerade, an Altar, & a Fairy (An Enlighten Series Novella)*. I have to tell you, I really love Sidelle. She was my favorite to write about. Many readers have told me: "We want to know why Shay and not Kieran?" Well, stay tuned because Kieran's story isn't over. He will have his own Novella. How did he become the bossy and take-charge Guardian angel?

When I wrote *The Masquerade, an Altar, & a Fairy (An Enlighten Series Novella)*, I received many comments from readers thanking me for sharing Sidelle's story. Some had an opinion about her and Finn, while others rooted for something to happen with her and Kieran? As an author, I love feedback! Candidly you are the reason that I will explore maybe doing more short stories, possibly one of Aiden or Cali. So tell me what you liked, what you loved, and even what you hated. I'd love to hear from you. You can write to me kristinvanrisseghem@msn.com, visit me on the web at www.KristinVanRisseghem.com, follow me on @KVanRisseghem, and like my Facebook Author Page www.facebook.com/KristinDVanRisseghem.Author.

I encourage you to keep at it. Keep going and looking ahead. And remember that you can do it! Find beta readers, critique partners and join writing groups. If some aren't working out, don't be afraid to find new ones. I found a slew of writers on Facebook, Twitter and Meetup.

Finally, I need to ask a favor. If you're so inclined I'd love a review of *The Masquerade, an Altar, & a Fairy (An Enlighten Series Novella)*. Loved it, hated it – I just enjoy your feedback.

As you may have gleaned from my book, reviews can be tough to come by these days. You, the reader, have the power now to make or break a book. If you have the time, please go to Amazon and leave a review.

Thank you so much for reading *The Masquerade, an Altar, & a Fairy (An Enlighten Series Novella)* and for spending time with me.

Sincerely,
Kristin D. Van Risseghem, Author